The
SIGNORE

Shogun of the Warring States

Kunio Tsuji

Translated by Stephen Snyder

KODANSHA INTERNATIONAL
Tokyo and New York

Originally published in 1968 by Chikuma Shobo under the title *Azuchi Okanki.*

Publication of this translation was assisted by a grant from the Japan Foundation.

Distributed in the United States by Kodansha International/ USA Ltd., 114 Fifth Avenue, New York, New York 10011. Published by Kodansha International Ltd., 17-14, Otowa 1-chome, Bunkyo-ku, Tokyo 112 and Kodansha International/ USA Ltd. Copyright © 1989 by Kodansha International Ltd. All rights reserved. Printed in Japan.
                              ISBN 4-7700-1439-2 (in Japan)
First edition, 1989

Library of Congress Cataloging-in-Publication Data
Tsuji, Kunio, 1925–
   [Azuchi okanki. English]
   The signore : shogun of the warring states / Kunio Tsuji : translated by Stephen Snyder. — 1st ed.
      p. cm
   Translation of: Azuchi okanki.
   ISBN 0-87011-939-7 (U.S.)
   1. Japan—History—Azuchi Momoyama period, 1568-1603—Fiction. 2. Japan—Church history—To 1868—Fiction. I. Title.
PL862.S73A9813   1989
895.6'35—dc20   89-45167

To the late Arimasa Mori

PREFACE

The historical novel, more than other genres, requires of its reader a certain background in order to be fully understood. Working within a particular cultural tradition, an author generally assumes a shared knowledge of basic events and figures. The novelist takes this knowledge and expands it or turns it on its head, depending on his intentions or predilections; yet always, in the final analysis, he makes his point in relation to what the reader knew to start with. Thus, Tolstoy's characterization of Napoleon differs from his characterization of Pierre, for in the latter case we have only what Tolstoy gives us, while in the former we inevitably compare his account with our preconceived notions of who Napoleon was and what he did. Without the background, some of the meaning is lost.

The Japanese reader of Tsuji Kunio's novel would quickly identify the "Signore" as Oda Nobunaga, a name (though the name itself, by design, is never mentioned) that summons up certain images from a collective Japanese cultural consciousness. These images—or preconceptions, or prejudices—become, in a sense, the ground on which the novelist paints his picture and which the non-Japanese reader, too, must understand to some extent in order to fully appreciate the novel.

Oda Nobunaga, youthful chieftain of the parvenu Oda clan, rulers of the relatively insignificant province of Owari, was the unlikely figure to whom fell the task of reunifying Japan after more than two centuries of continuous civil war. To accomplish this, he had to subdue or destroy the twenty or so more powerful warlords or *daimyo* who survived the Onin War, many of whom—

Takeda Shingen of Kai and Uesugi Kenshin of Echigo, for example—had their own plans for establishing hegemony in the divided country. For more than twenty years, from his rise to power in Owari in 1559 to his death in 1582, Nobunaga battled these rival lords, first singly then later in various "stop Nobunaga" alliances. Also opposing him was a formidable army of soldier-monks fielded by the militant Ikko sect of Buddhism, which maintained monastic strongholds throughout the country and harbored a deep-seated dislike for the young, avowedly irreligious warlord. The history of Nobunaga's struggles against these enemies, which forms the central plot of *The Signore*, is a complex tale full of twists and surprises, setbacks and brilliant victories; but in the end Nobunaga was successful. From a precarious position as lord of a minor fief, he rose to virtually undisputed mastery of the central, and most significant, portion of Japan, and left at his death a political legacy around which his successors, Toyotomi Hideyoshi and Tokugawa Ieyasu, were able to create the modern Japanese state.

The Japanese reader would be familiar with this biographical outline. In much the same way the reader of *War and Peace* has at least a vague notion of Napoleon's campaigns in Europe and his frustrated attempt to subdue Russia. In addition, though, Tolstoy would expect his reader to come armed with some simple notions about Napoleon's character—that he was, for example, overbearing and not a little vain. Similarly, in Nobunaga's case the popular—and, indeed, the academic—image tends to focus on the means he used to achieve his dramatically successful ends; specifically, there is a fair degree of unanimity in condemning those means as unnecessarily ruthless.

The details of the acts which earned Nobunaga this reputation are vividly described in this book, and need not be retold here; instead, three variants of a *haiku*, familiar to most Japanese, will give some idea of how he is remembered by his countrymen. The poems describe how the three founders of the Japanese nation would have dealt with a cuckoo that refused to sing. Toyotomi Hideyoshi, Nobunaga's successor and a brilliant military strategist, demonstrates his resourcefulness:

nakanunaraba	If the cuckoo
nakashite miyo	will not sing,
hototogisu	try to make it sing.

Tokugawa Ieyasu, who followed Hideyoshi and established the stable, long-lived Tokugawa shogunate, displays characteristic patience:

nakanunaraba	If the cuckoo
naku made mato	will not sing,
hototogisu	wait till it sings.

But Nobunaga's poem says simply:

nakanunaraba	If the cuckoo
koroshite shimae	will not sing,
hototogisu	kill it.

Unfortunately for Nobunaga, historians are not much kinder than the makers of popular jingles; while a few apologists try to justify his activities, most agree with Sir George Sansom's indictment in his *History of Japan*:

> If his virtues are open to doubt, his vices are unquestionable. He never showed a sign of compassion. His vindictive ruthlessness is apparent from the beginning of his career, when he murdered his brother, to his last years, which were filled with wanton slaughter. He became the master of twenty provinces at a terrible cost. He was a cruel and callous brute.
>
> [volume 2, p. 310]

Tsuji Kunio is well aware that readers bring to his novel an idea of his protagonist as a "cruel and callous brute"; and, brilliantly, he responds to their preconceptions by creating a narrator who is free from such notions. *The Signore* is told in the words of an Italian adventurer who comes to Japan in the company of Jesuit missionaries and whose impressions of and, later, friendship with the Signore develop, if not in ignorance of, then wholly independently of, the prevailing view. Like the Jesuit missionaries upon whose records portions of Tsuji's work are based, the narrator (who remains nameless and is, in fact, the only nonhistorical character in the novel) sees a gentler, more contemplative—even lonely—side of Nobunaga, a side he carefully conceals from his subjects for fear it could be seen as weakness. Free from local prejudices and largely innocent of the convoluted politics of the Japanese kingdom, the narrator forms his own opinions of events and the actors in them. In his eyes, the "callous brute" becomes a tragic figure, an intensely curious and utterly rational man condemned to isolation by his relentless adherence to one absolute standard of human behavior.

The Nobunaga who emerges in Tsuji's portrait, the Nobunaga to be measured against the one in the *haiku* or the history books, is a complex character, part Renaissance man (as the narrator projects something of his self-image on the Japanese lord), part existentialist hero (here the author's extensive knowledge of French literature makes itself apparent), and, in the end, wholly human. It is in this last respect that *The Signore* succeeds in doing what good historical novels do best: that is, to bring to life a figure who existed previously only in flat, factual accounts.

I would like to thank those who gave their time and expertise to help with this translation. I am grateful to the author for his encouragement and for his understanding of the nature of the translation process. Moriyasu Machiko of Kodansha International tracked down information on everything from medieval firearms to kimono styles and generally made things easier. Nakamura Fumiko and Nakamura Akiko answered many questions in the later stages of the work. Stephen Shaw, also of Kodansha, offered sound editorial advice and John Bester was kind enough to read the entire manuscript and make many needed improvements. Finally, Linda White worked with me in the early stages, encouraged me in the later ones, and throughout was both best critic and best friend. Any difficulties which may remain are, of course, solely my responsibility.

Stephen Snyder

Note: Names (except on the title and dedication pages) are given in the Japanese order, family or clan name first. The vassal referred to as Hashiba is Nobunaga's above-mentioned successor, Toyotomi Hideyoshi, who changed his name several times during his life.

THE SIGNORE

I

℗ he lengthy letter translated herein was discovered in the collection of Monsieur C. Rouziès, a noted bibliophile from the city of Rodez in southern France. The manuscript, believed to be in the hand of the original author, was found inserted in the back of a volume of unrelated works. The letter is written in Italian, but I have based this translation on a French version done by M. Rouziès.

The manuscript itself has already been the subject of several studies. The handwriting of the first one hundred and fifty pages has been carefully compared with that in the manuscript entitled "Record of the Japanese Envoy to Rome in the Year 1582" by Diego de Mesquita which was found bound together with the manuscript of Luis Frois's "History of Japan" (also known as the Saldas Manuscript A) discovered by Dorotheus Schilling in 1931; all studies conclude, however, that the present work is in a different hand. The script of the latter one hundred and fifty leaves is presently being compared with manuscripts from the archives of the Jesuit mission to Japan preserved in the Ajuda Library in Lisbon, but as yet no conjecture can be made as to the name of the author or the title of the current work.

It seems highly probable that additional copies of manuscripts dealing with Japan will be found in the near future in the Jesuit archives in Rome, in the National Library in Madrid, in the San Lorenzo Library in Escorial, or in other collections. The fact that Schilling discovered two copies of Frois's "History" almost simultaneously in the collection of Paul Saldas and in the Archivo

Historico Colonial in Lisbon suggests that a large number of manuscripts are extant and that further revelations are likely. I am, however, reasonably certain that no additional copies of this particular letter will come to light. Several factors argue in favor of such a conclusion. First, the writer of the letter had little or nothing to do with the work of the mission. He was not a member of the Jesuit order, and is occasionally quite critical of the church. This unidentified Italian belonged, rather, to a more anomalous brotherhood which flourished in the sixteenth century, that of seafaring adventurers. Second, the letter was not intended as a report to an official body, being more personal and private in nature. Thus the Jesuit clergy of the period would have tended to view it as essentially worthless. Third, for reasons unknown—the writer's illness or death perhaps—this Rouziès manuscript letter never reached its intended destination but was left where it was written, at the San Paolo Seminary in Goa on the western coast of India. We can only speculate that subsequently it was accidentally mixed in with other documents and eventually inserted into the volume in which it was found. Finally, even the language in which the letter is written makes the discovery of additional copies unlikely; such documents are written almost exclusively in Portuguese or Spanish, and the fact that it is in Italian underlines its uniqueness.

These factors suggesting that no additional copies will be found are, however, precisely what encouraged me to undertake this translation. The works of this kind that have been translated up to this point are all careful, factual reports by Jesuit missionaries. The present letter, it seems to me, provides a vivid portrait of sixteenth-century Japan from a very different point of view.

In conclusion, I should add a word of caution: the author of this letter was a man who witnessed the birth of Japan as a unified nation. If the significance of his experience is only faintly conveyed in these pages, the reader should not fault the author or his previous translator, but the limited historical knowledge and imagination of the present translator.

II

I can no longer recall with certainty in what year I last wrote to you. I believe it was in fifteen hundred and seventy-three, or perhaps the year after. If I remember correctly, I wrote at length about the passage from Malacca to the kingdom of Japan. Before going on to describe that land, I should tell you that recently, in the last year and a half since coming here to Goa, I chanced for the first time upon a copy of your book *A Comparison of the Forms of Statecraft in the Principalities of Florence, Venice, and Naples.* I confess to an inordinate pleasure on finding that you had been so kind as to include therein almost the whole of the account I sent you of my wanderings in Nuova Spagna and as far as the Molucca Islands.

I was delighted for a number of reasons. First, because I know better than most the uncertain fate of letters entrusted to those unreliable Portuguese ships; even as I wrote my usual long epistle, I had doubts that it would ever reach you. My delight was compounded by your kind words of acknowledgment: "a record from a friend, B. F. . . ." Most of all, though, I was happy because I felt that in including my journal in the book you were, in a sense, answering my letters. No doubt you have sent other, more conventional replies as well. Equally doubtless, though, you knew that the chance of such letters reaching me on my wanderings through distant lands was at best remote, so that it occurred to you to include in your book those several paragraphs which could only have been a message to me—reasoning, I assume, that a printed book which passes before so many eyes had a better chance of finding its way to mine. Your reasoning was sound. I am certain now that my records reached you, and—more gratifying still—that you read them with pleasure.

I trust too that you received the letter I wrote from Hirado. Since then, I have had neither time nor inclination to keep such records. I was, in truth, quite overwhelmed by the events I witnessed in the years that followed my last letter. Though, in all the time I spent in the kingdom of Japan, I came to know only a fraction of what there was to know, and though even that fraction seems to me puzzling and uncommonly complex, it is also true that I felt there, perhaps for the first time in my life, that I might have discovered some value in human existence.

In Nuova Spagna, as you know, I served as an officer under the governor Ibarra. It was at his orders that I marched for weeks through parched valleys, under a scorching sun, to put down an insurrection. My troops suffered sorely from the heat and humidity, from fever and hunger. As we cut our way through tangled swamps, I would see the healthy glow gradually drain from the cheeks of young recruits, till they looked like jaundiced skeletons and moved like old men; in the end, they would be stumbling along, moaning and gasping, like marionettes formed from the mud itself. Yet I remained faithful to the governor's orders, and though our numbers shrank by half from desertion, disease, and drownings, I refused to turn back, for I viewed this suffering as a kind of challenge from my destiny.

Once these deeds were done, moreover, a similar desire to do battle with fate took me to sea. True, disillusionment with the lot of the conquistador played a part in my decision to leave the army and join a Spanish fleet sailing for the Molucca Islands. But I can see now that the urge I had to pursue my destiny wherever it might lead was still more important. And I can bear witness too that the mighty Pacific does not disappoint the man who chases after destiny, for its vast, endless expanse is the very mirror of fate itself. I have spent ten years at sea, yet to this day I cannot hear with equanimity the creaking of the mast before a storm. I cannot bear to watch the flight of black clouds across the sky, or feel the swelling of the waves. At such moments, a cold weight sits heavily on my chest and my heart is troubled. And there is something unspeakably disheartening in the sight of that ultimate, desolate sea at the end of a month's sail unbroken by any glimpse of land; one feels that the ship has come to the end of the earth, there perforce to await, becalmed, for the wind. At such times, even the hardiest sea dog regrets that he ever undertook such a reckless voyage. Yet it was for just such moments that I chose (if the word applies here) the life of a sailor: only such moments, I felt, could satisfy me of my true will to do battle with destiny.

You are not unaware, friend, of how "destiny" has plagued me ever since that fateful moment when I killed my wife and her lover in an alley of Genoa. At the instant my crime was accomplished, when I first came to see clearly the circumstances in which I had been trapped, I resolved not to submit but to fight in every way to overcome blind destiny. And my resistance began— arbitrarily enough, perhaps—with a resolve not to submit to the law and customs, or the gloomy materialism, of our native city. In short, I fled.

I do not think I am deceiving myself when I say that this resolve was something more than an excuse to escape justice and save my life. Even now I see a very different kind of justice at work in these dealings. It seems to me that, in the natural order of things, the treachery practiced by my wife and that man required their deaths in expiation, and that the redemption bought with their lives was not for me personally but for love itself. To see my act as a crime, to submit to the law, would have been, I believe, to besmirch love itself and, with it, my self-respect as a human being. By the same token, to conclude simply that my deed had been involuntary—or, worse, imposed on me by a sinister fate— would have been to deny my freedom to act or to feel the strong

7

feelings that prompted my actions. I killed my wife and her lover in the violence of my love; yet my deed was a free choice made of my own will.

Fleeing Genoa, I made my way to Lisbon. There I worked as a porter, sleeping in a corner of a warehouse on the docks. I wandered about the city like a vagrant: whipped on occasion by passing coachmen, laughed at by ladies in the street. I learned to grovel, and to beg in the grog shops; nor was I above stealing in the markets. So you see, my friend, I was not only a murderer but a beggar and a thief as well. I took my place among the lowest of the low. Yet, inasmuch as I had chosen all these things of my free will, I remained true, I told myself, to my resolve to resist the iron hand of fate. This, indeed, became my new obsession: to the point of convincing myself that, far from being overpowered by fate, I was its master. I had stopped being driven. I had taken the reins in my own hands, and was pushing ahead step by step in the direction of my choosing. Or so it seemed to me. At the same time this meant, however, that I was obliged to do mental battle with destiny at every waking moment. To stumble an instant, to become frightened, to lose confidence would, I feared, turn the tables and allow destiny in triumph to seize me and shake me by the throat.

A peculiar consequence of this way of viewing things was a compulsion to see even the worst of my misadventures and misfortunes as things I had willed, even greatly desired. If I tripped on a stone in the street, it was because I had wished to do so. If a coachman chose to whip me and rob me of all I had, it must be the product of my volition. It was an odd race—no matter how circumstances attempted to overtake me, I surged frantically ahead crying "No! I have willed it all to happen!"

Again, when I signed on in Lisbon to sail to the New World, I told myself, protecting my pride, that I was not running away but accepting a challenge. Not that it was simply to gratify this peculiar vanity that I went to seek distant lands. It was, rather, that I sensed something within me that had to be guarded with the greatest care. My life was to be a long struggle for some sort of integrity. It was that struggle that led me, after many vicissitudes, to the unexpected shores of Japan; and the same struggle determined that I should remain there. When I review all these circumstances now, from this distance in time and space, I must tell you, my friend, I am still filled with a kind of awe.

By virtue of my long sojourn in Japan, I have acquired a certain mastery of that mellifluous Eastern tongue which I am at present teaching to priests preparing for the mission field. I live and teach here at the seminary of San Paolo. From my room, I can see the strong walls that circle Goa in a band of shining white. As I write, the burning sun casts deep shadows in alleys where donkeys stand, heads bowed to the afternoon heat. A guard on the rampart is no more than a black speck as he paces out his watch; he, at least, will feel the breeze from the sea. Above the gray roofs of the town, I can see the Church of San Francisco and the palace of the viceroys of India. The buildings and the narrow streets crammed between them crowd our tiny island. Across the straits, the kingdom of Goa and the crumbling dome of a mosque are visible against the pale blue mountains.

We have no winter here, nor any true spring or autumn. The heat of eternal summer hangs in a bright haze over the aqua sea. Here the hours pass slowly, heavily. While the sun is still low, the sound of women's voices drifts up from the well at the foot of the hill below the seminary. But soon, they too are quiet, and only the droning of flies and the murmur of the distant sea disturb the silence of my darkened room.

No Portuguese ship has called here these past three months. There is no word yet of the *Santa Maria*, which is now overdue. In any case, I fear its arrival would prove scant comfort. I have grown weary: of heat and idleness, but most of all of a gaping void

9

inside me that will not be filled. The feeling has long troubled me; I first felt it while I was in the kingdom of Japan, and it haunts me to this day. The feeling is most disheartening. There are times when I would like to make studies of the government and customs of Japan to send to you—but the emptiness deprives me of the will for such labors. The most I can hope for is the strength to write to you of something ineffable that I feel I have lost, while there yet remains a vestige of that which I once discovered in this vain life. . . .

I first landed in that kingdom early in the summer of fifteen hundred and seventy. As the lighter from the ship neared the shore, we saw people running onto the beach to welcome us, carrying a cross. Several of them clutched rosaries, and their expressions bespoke the importance of the occasion for them. I was among the first landing party, since I had been given responsibility for seeing Father Cabral and Father Organtino safely to this kingdom where they were to continue the work of evangelizing the heathens.

The village where we had landed was called Kuchinotsu, a tidy, peaceful hamlet on a calm inlet. The village of Shiki, which we visited later, was another similar settlement. At Shiki, there were several Japanese friars who were quite fluent in Portuguese, and a small church stood a short distance from the village. My first impression of the Japanese was of a fair-skinned, courteous people who smiled readily and were extremely clean in their persons. Nor later did I have much cause to revise this opinion, except insofar as the courtesy and affability of the Japanese is not infrequently tempered with a kind of contempt or condescension, a combination not generally seen among the peoples of Europe.

At the back of the church at Shiki, in a room sunk deep in shadows, Father Torres lay on his sickbed. He had come to this kingdom with the first mission led by Francis Xavier—that most politically minded father—who by now was managing church affairs in Goa and Malacca. For the past twenty years, I was told, Torres had lived on a meager diet of rice, dried radishes, and vegetable gruel; he had been pelted by storms, driven from home by civil disturbances, attacked by monks of the religious order known as Buddhism, and abused by villagers. In spite of all this, he had finally established this single parish in Shimo island (which is also known as Kyushu), and had even journeyed as far as the capital. Now, at the news of the arrival of Fathers Cabral and Organtino, he seemed to rally a little, and wept for joy at the sight of his fellows.

"Welcome! Welcome!" the old man murmured. His face, so sunburnt and wrinkled that it was no longer recognizable as that of a white man, was damp with tears. Without delay, he began to express regret at what he saw as his failure to fulfill the hopes that the Secretary General of the order and the other brothers had pinned on this land where Christ was yet unknown.

It was a kingdom, he told us, plagued with strife, ignorance, and prejudice. "I am old and sick," he said. "Never again will I go out into the streets to call the people to the faith. Little has been accomplished, and I have grown feeble. Yet even that is not my chief sorrow; I have a more practical concern to share with you, my brothers. Father Frois has been left alone in Miyako, the capital of this land—left all alone to shepherd the souls of believers there. I would be most comforted if someone could go quickly to assist him. There is a great need of fathers in the capital. Brothers! I entreat you, dispatch someone to Miyako!"

Before we had been long in Shiki, I had heard old Torres utter these or similar words more than a few times. It may be that his mind was failing, yet even as he weakened he still clung to this long-cherished desire to help his colleague in the capital. Whenever anyone came, he repeated his request almost deliriously. And in the end, he was successful, for it was no doubt due in some measure to the urgency of his entreaties that Father Cabral decided to send Organtino to Miyako, the capital, even though the latter had yet to recover completely from the illnesses that had plagued him on the voyage out.

Father Torres died on the second of October, four months after our arrival. The corpse, burnt brown by the sun and shriveled with age, seemed to have shrunk from life and grown stiff much as a mummy does. The dark, sunken eyes suggested the exquisite peace of a soul freed from a long agony. Yet as I sat contemplating the face of this old man, I found myself for some reason thinking of Organtino.

Father Organtino Gnecchi-Soldi was, in his own way, another remarkable man. He was born into a peasant family in the hills of Brescia, not so far from our own Genoa. Cheerful and carefree by nature, he had the portliness often associated with such a disposition. He lacked, however, the constitution to match his frame, being in fact rather frail. On the voyage from Goa, he had suffered from seasickness, sunstroke, and colic, and had spent much of his time below deck. That he managed through all this to observe his daily Christian offices was no doubt related to the fact that he was traveling with the chief of the mission to the parish of Japan, Vice-Provincial Francisco Cabral.

Cabral himself was an aristocrat. Strict, even harsh by nature, he was not the sort to view others with indulgence. He was almost menacingly tall, with piercing gray eyes and an aquiline nose. His lips were slightly drawn, and his skin had been burned brown on the long voyage through the South Seas. All in all, his appearance suggested an ascetically minded medieval warrior rather than a priest. He was fond of railing at the sailors—myself included—as the most depraved men on the face of the earth; you will easily infer that I never developed much liking for him. I recognized, nevertheless, an unusual spiritual strength and a special gift for moral discourse and sermonizing. On the occasions when he exercised this gift, his eloquence was searing and his words conjured up vivid pictures of Hell, but his manner as he censored the sins of men was unnecessarily haughty.

Organtino was a different sort altogether. He was a man of the people, a man who invited confidences. He was a friendly soul who accepted one and all—even the likes of me, though I was in no sense a believer nor likely to become one. His round eyes greeted everyone with a kindly look. Perhaps because his birthplace was near my own, I had taken a great liking to him from the moment we met in Goa. Later, when I got myself into a bad scrape over gambling and wounded three of my opponents in a fight, it was he who with great difficulty rescued me and smoothed over the whole affair. Without his assistance, I would at the very least have been left behind by the ship, and might well have ended up in a penal colony on one of the Molucca Islands. I will confess that strong drink was to blame for this little incident.

The voyage from Goa had dragged on for several months, during which Organtino succumbed to one complaint after another, each seemingly worse than the last. I was in almost constant attendance upon him until we reached Japan, and it was a lingering concern for his health that had led me to accompany him as far as Shiki.

Thus it was that I was present when Father Torres died. At the news of his death, the Japanese Christians threw themselves weeping on the floor of their church, and the bell tolled solemnly across the harbor.

Yet—to return to my subject—I cannot say that in Torres's brown face, wrinkled skin, and sunken eyes I saw the features of a man who had lived life to the full; rather, I saw one who had labored under a constant sense of debt to someone or something, whose life had been tortured and fearful. Oddly enough, though, the face had something in common—what exactly, I could not say—with the friendly, good-natured features of Organtino. Something in it called to mind the wry little smile that would flutter across Organtino's face even when he was deathly seasick, and the way he would try, even then, to find some joke to amuse me.

I need hardly tell you, my friend, that I was not one to spend much time delving into the spiritual complexities of these men who chose to go off evangelizing foreign lands—though I was quite sure that they were not to be pitied, not by the likes of me at any rate. While I found it strangely troubling to witness the spiritual sufferings that Torres and Organtino endured on account of their single-minded devotion, I remained puzzled by such blind faith. It reminded me of the look of trust I had once seen on the face of a dog pierced by an errant arrow from its own master's bow. Dying, it had tottered toward its master: mute, bewildered, dragging its entrails, yet with eyes full of silent faith.

Unfortunately, Organtino was soon to be given a chance to demonstrate this kind of faith, for on his way back to Kuchinotsu from Shiki he was attacked and beaten by a group of heathens. It was, in fact, this event that determined me on a course of action. I had been having certain difficulties with the captain of my ship. Moreover, now that the fathers were safely ashore, I had no specific duties for the return voyage. On the other hand, I had no particular reason at that point to stay in Japan, but the blood-smeared face of Organtino as he was carried into the church made up my mind for me. Though I still lacked any proper pretext for remaining with the fathers, I was suddenly determined, at the very least, to see this child of Brescia as far as the capital.

The attack on Organtino had an effect on others in our party as well. For Father Cabral, it only confirmed the opinion that, with all the arrogance of a newcomer, he had conceived at the outset: that there was no difference between the natives of this kingdom and those in the environs of Goa or Malacca. He clung to this view despite all the accounts of the virtues of this country that had been sent to the San Paolo seminary by Fathers Xavier, Torres, and Vilela. He declined to take his meals with the Japanese friars, let alone with the ordinary parishioners, and his manner of living was little different from that of a Portuguese nobleman. His table never lacked for meat or cheese or wine, which is all the more remarkable when one notes how Torres had subsisted on rice, a little millet, and dried radish, and had kept company with peasants and vagrants.

But I digress. Even after his misadventure, Organtino was not at all inclined to accept my offer to accompany him. For some time he had been urging me to return home as soon as possible, and when I told him that I would like to see him as far as Miyako he merely repeated the same advice.

"The land of our birth has changed greatly during the past few years. Do you not wish to see it once again? Still more to the point, my friend—though you offer to accompany me as a guard, there is nothing whatsoever about you that would be likely to frighten off an attacker."

I did not answer him but led him around to the back of the church, to a vegetable garden of some forty square yards, bordered on one side by a stone wall. On the wall I propped up a silver medallion, engraved with a likeness of the patron saint of Genoa, that I carried with me. Walking fifty paces from the wall, I took my arquebus from my haversack, loaded it, aimed, and pulled the trigger. The gun roared and the silver disk danced up into the air. I recovered what was left of it and presented it to Organtino.

"Please observe," I said. "This is all that remains of Genoa for me, and I have no course left but to go with you." I may have mentioned in a previous letter that while I was in Nuova Spagna I studied not only surveying and the science of fortification but marksmanship as well. At one time, I was so intent on it that I developed the ability to hit a Spanish gold piece at fifty paces.

As I had hoped, Organtino was immensely impressed:

"And where, may I inquire, did a sailor learn such a trick?"

Nevertheless, even after this demonstration, he was still reluctant to let me go with him. In the end, he suffered my company on condition that I was to go only as far as the capital, extracting a promise from me that as soon as the Portuguese ship arrived the following year, I would board it and make a quick passage home to Europe. At the time I did not feel I would be unwilling to keep such a promise.

I was not party to any of the meetings held to discuss the subject of Organtino's mission to the capital, nor do I know what orders Father Cabral had himself received in this regard. I know only that Organtino, though less than fully recovered from his illness, was instructed to depart shortly after the funeral of Father Torres. In addition to the two of us, our party consisted of two Japanese friars and about five men to carry our baggage. We set out by boat from Kuchinotsu, and after a long delay in Hirado continued overland to Funai where we once more put to sea.

The journey was for the most part uneventful, though with an occasional unpleasant turn of events. One of the other passengers on the boat from Funai told the boatman that he would not sail with heathens and that we should have been refused passage. At this, a woman great with child shrieked that her baby would surely be born a monster as punishment for traveling with infidels, and urged that we be thrown in the sea straightway. On two or three occasions a group of men approached us, plainly bent on starting trouble, but things never went so far that I had to produce my gun. Others of the passengers were in fact quite kind, including one old woman who offered to share with us her lunch of rice wrapped in leaves.

During the trip, Organtino talked about the kingdom of Japan through which we were passing. It was not the first time I had heard him hold forth on this topic. On the long voyage from Goa he had talked with almost feverish intensity, his information drawn from the voluminous reports sent from Miyako or Bungo to Goa and Coimbra by his predecessors: Gaspar Vilela, Luis Frois, Luis de Almeida, and others who had been to the capital after Torres. In addition to their work at the mission, these men had made diligent studies of the kingdom: its history, customs, manners, food, dress, architecture, politics, administrative organization, geography, and most especially the religion known as Buddhism.

However, it was only during our passage through this peaceful inland sea that I really began to take in what Organtino was saying. He used many words that were unfamiliar to my ears—"Danjo," "Kubo-sama," and the like—but eventually it became apparent that these were the names of powerful men who were at present the source of considerable strife in the capital. Organtino spoke of the politics of the kingdom with a great deal of intensity, though it hardly seems likely to me now that, at that early point in our stay, he could have understood all the details of its enmities and alliances.

After ten days at sea, we arrived at Sakai. The harbor was protected by a breakwater made of stone, at the end of which a beacon light had been erected. The harbor itself was filled with ships and boats, colorful flags flying from their masts as they plied the waters in and out of the port. Everywhere there was tremendous activity; ships were being made fast to the docks or jostling one another for position, men were shouting and bells ringing. As we approached the pier, we could see someone waiting for us. This was Brother Lorenzo, a short, somewhat swarthy old man who was lame, quite blind in one eye, and all but blind in the other.

Organtino had already told me a good deal about this Japanese monk. He had been one of the very first Japanese converts to Christianity. Becoming a friar, he had devoted himself to the work of the mission, sharing Father Torres's trials with him.

When we told him of the latter's death, tears welled up in his sunken and nearly sightless eyes.

We were led to the imposing residence of a merchant situated on the main street of Sakai. The owner, an influential tradesman who sat on the city council, proved to be a portly, self-satisfied character whose crafty, evasive manner reminded me of the bankers and burghers of Genoa. In fact, the similarities between the leading citizens of Sakai and their counterparts in our native city struck me more and more as time passed. They were haughty, even arrogant men. Every article of their clothing was the finest to be had, and something about them suggested a special type of worldliness and devotion to the pursuit of sensual pleasures. I need hardly tell you, my friend, that far from inducing in me nostalgia or homesickness, these similarities provoked a certain repugnance. The town, it struck me, had just the kind of atmosphere that had prompted my wife to be unfaithful.

For a time, however, I was obliged to live with these feelings, and Organtino to forego his urgent desire to press on to the capital. In the end, we were unable to leave Sakai immediately, for Lorenzo had come not simply to welcome us, but also to bid us stay awhile. The capital, he told us, was in a state of dire turmoil, with two opposing forces locked in battle for its control. District after district was being plundered and whole villages on the outskirts of the city had been burned. Black smoke, he said, blanketed the sky continually, while mounted soldiers, sinister figures, roved the streets. The whole city was in a panic; amidst the frantic tolling of bells, citizens were fleeing their homes, the fortunate carrying off what they could in carts while others buried their treasures in the ground and escaped with just their lives, leaving the rest to weep and moan helplessly in the streets.

"Is Padre Frois still in the capital?" Organtino interrupted, raising his voice in spite of himself.

"He is," replied Lorenzo. "It is at times such as these that the faithful have most need of him. He has been specially to the court to petition the king for protection for the church, and he has been comforting the faithful in every part of the city. He has reopened the abandoned sanctuary, and is using the old ritual implements to hold Mass. If Padre Frois were to leave Miyako now, our people would be deprived of their chief buttress, and the church that we built at such great pains would surely crumble. That is why—" Lorenzo hurried on as though to prevent Organtino from interrupting again "—the padre has sent me here. As one who has worked side by side with him, I feel I may be frank. He has asked me to say that you would be of little use to him in the capital while you are still unable to speak the language and have no knowledge of the situation here. He feels that you should first gain some skill in the Japanese tongue, and a thorough understanding of political matters. We ask, therefore, that you should stay for a time in this city with me."

Organtino hesitated. "Such a suggestion is contrary to my instructions from the Vice Provincial, Father Cabral. He is the chief of this mission and he has bidden me to proceed without delay. . . ."

"We fully realize that what we are asking is against the terms of your commission. That is precisely why the padre has sent me. For some time now we have been hearing of Padre Cabral's splendid discernment and his strong will. Nevertheless, you must remember that he is only lately arrived in this country and has not himself witnessed the turmoil that has suddenly embroiled the capital. Dare I suggest that he cannot possibly view matters as clearly as Padre Frois. I beg you then to yield to the padre's request and remain here in Sakai. We will take full responsibility for the consequences."

In the end, there was nothing for it but to stay awhile in Sakai. We had some slight consolation in the fact that the city was, at least, a very safe place for us to be at that moment. It was surrounded by a deep moat backed by high walls, and entry was to be gained only through the sturdy city gates. The bridges over the moat were drawn up at night, and the guardhouses were manned by mercenaries. Indeed, the fortifications seemed almost to rival those of Venice. Another, perhaps more important, circumstance contributing to our well-being was the fact that the citizens of Sakai, as we were told, bore no ill will toward Christians.

Wandering about, we gained an idea of the layout of the city. Two broad streets intersected at its center, the quarters thus formed being checkered with smaller lanes. The great avenues were lined with magnificent shops and bustling markets. Along the waterfront stood rice and fish markets, boatyards, and lumberyards. The streets were crowded with people, some hurrying along, others loading and unloading their carts, doing business, or merely talking idly. I saw all kinds of trades on my walks through the city: blacksmiths, purveyors of dyed goods and yarns, apothecaries, moneylenders, and printers who worked from wooden blocks. Most interesting to me, though, were the swordsmiths and gunsmiths whose shops lined the streets in the northern quarters. Here, hot fires burned and workers were busy beating sheets of steel and bending iron bars. Beyond the smithies, at the northernmost edge of town, was a dusty field, overgrown with weeds, where the makers of guns tested their muskets on targets set up against a crumbling mud wall.

When Lorenzo began taking us around the city, I soon noticed that the citizens all seemed to be in an abnormally great hurry. They were, I learned, doing brisk business thanks to the war being fought in the capital. The smiths especially were working day and night, running their shops in shifts, the bellows pumping and the hammers beating seemingly without respite. Carts stacked high with goods rolled back and forth between the harbor and the storehouses, and the entire population of Sakai rushed about as if possessed by demons.

In the course of our wanderings, we managed to stop a few passers-by long enough to ask why they were all so busy. Their answers, given with a mixture of urgency and annoyance, were always the same: the Lord of Owari was spending enormous sums on supplies and munitions for his campaign, and there was money to be made. When we pressed to know who this Lord of Owari was and what sort of man he might be, the answer again was always the same: he was the most brutal and heartless warlord who had ever lived. One merchant told us with a scowl that the Lord of Owari had murdered his own brother, banished his uncle, and slaughtered many of his own vassals. What is more, he assured us, the man actually enjoyed the carnage.

"When this lord makes war," he continued, "he has no thought of mercy, but sees to it that his enemy is eliminated to the last man. He has burned a great many towns, and he destroys the temples of the Buddha. He is under the spell of some evil spirit—perhaps he is a devil himself. The very thought of him makes me shiver. . . . When he came here to Sakai to demand a contribution of twenty thousand *kan* for his war chest, the town council flatly refused him. We drew up the bridges, barred the gates, and set up fortifications; every last soul was prepared to take arms to defend the city. But it was worse than hopeless. The Lord of Owari had fifty thousand soldiers waiting at the capital for the least pretext to attack us. The lords of Miyoshi and Tango, harsh though they were, were never half so cruel as this Owari. At his coming, the gods themselves are put to flight and the Buddhas vanish, leaving only burning and killing. In form he is a man, but in truth he is a fearsome monster!"

The merchant spoke quickly and with great agitation, glancing about him all the while as if the monster's approach were imminent. Then, abruptly, he fell silent and wandered away.

His performance left me astounded. Not even Cosimo de' Medici, I felt—not Nero, even, or Nebuchadnezzar—had inspired such fear and hatred as attended this Lord of Owari. Surely, he was even more despised than the bloodthirsty Hun! As the merchant spoke, I had a vision of a pale, grim face with a cold, perhaps slightly crazed expression. I could see him in my mind's eye: a small man—hunchbacked, perhaps, and lacking the fingers on one hand for good measure. The embodiment of evil, he stood gazing into the flames rising from the towns he had burned. . . . And then it occurred to me that the great Hernán Cortés and Francisco Pizarro had also been responsible for bloody massacres—not of mere tens or twenties, but of hundreds and thousands of people at a time. They too had burned villages—nay, whole cities. And I had an odd conviction that their deeds, too, must have shown on their faces. Even though such men might occasionally have managed to put on brave or cheerful faces, they could surely never have masked the foul deeds written on their souls. Was the Lord of Owari such a man—a man like Cortés or Pizarro? I began to wonder whether I would meet this infamous lord, and what sort of man he would prove to be. A brute? A tyrant? A desperado? Time and again, I fell to such musings as we waited in Sakai. . . .

Meanwhile, Organtino was devoting all his energies to learning the Japanese tongue under Lorenzo's tutelage. He had taken to delivering sermons to anyone who would listen, in the spacious room at the rear of the upper floor of the imposing mansion where we were lodged. After four months or so, he had progressed to the point where these sermons, with a bit of help from Lorenzo, were delivered in faltering Japanese. When we went about in the city, he would approach anyone he found standing idle and engage him in conversation. I, of course, could understand nothing of what was said at such times, but, oddly enough, the sound of Organtino's voice speaking this foreign tongue had the same comforting quality as when he spoke in the inimitable accents of Brescia. It seemed that those he approached were quite pleased to speak with him, and some of them, whether from pleasure or nervousness, actually laughed.

At first, when we walked the streets of Sakai, people would pause from their work; some came out of their houses to stare at us, and at times we were even followed about by a small crowd of women and children. However, by the time Organtino could speak to them in even the most broken Japanese, this bold curiosity had dwindled, and we finally reached the point where we were greeted in markets or shops by the nods and smiles of acquaintances rather than the curious stares of strangers.

It was during this period that I encountered a very wealthy member of the city council named Tzuda. He was a large, imposing man who appeared to be in his forties, with big, thick ears and eyes bulging from his head. Our meeting was indirectly due to the considerable impression made upon me by the advanced state of gunsmithing in the city. I had asked for a demonstration of the manufacturing processes then in use, and upon being refused— on the grounds that such information was regarded as secret—hit upon a scheme to circumvent the obstacle. I gave a demonstration of my own at the shooting range, displaying my skill with the arquebus for the benefit of the gun manufacturers, and my efforts, as I had anticipated, were rewarded with an immediate invitation to inspect their workshops. Tzuda was one of the merchants who dealt in the arms and ammunition manufactured there.

I was asked to repeat my earlier feats and shoot a small saké bottle with my arquebus (saké is the name the Japanese give to their wine). Tzuda, like the others present, seemed surprised at my skill. But it was plain that his curiosity was still more tickled by my gun itself, an Italian piece in a style quite new to him, the mere sight of which made his eyes sparkle. He asked me to explain the difference between my new arquebus and a musket. By way of answer, I opened the base of the gun and showed him the firing device, which employed a cogwheel with a spring attached to it. Then, to demonstrate the superior simplicity of the arquebus, I showed him how quickly and easily the ball and powder could be loaded. When I had done, Tzuda insisted that I be his guest at dinner.

His house was magnificent, surrounded by a high wall and a moat flowing with fresh water. The rooms were exceedingly numerous and separated each from the other by golden partitions. The corridors were lined with wooden doors decorated with paintings of flowers and animals. In the garden, there was a pond bordered with flowers and stones, and next to it a small knoll topped by a pavilion.

During the banquet that evening, Tzuda asked about current conditions in trade between Goa and Macao, explaining that he would like to import quantities of saltpeter from the latter. I on my side told him that before coming to Japan I could never have imagined that firearms were so highly developed and widely used there.

"I have been wondering," I continued, "to which of the lords and generals you sell your guns." The question evoked a vague half-smile that I recognized immediately as the mark of cunning worn by men of affairs the world over when they are preparing to do business. At the same time, it was slightly different; somehow, it was more unfounded, more meaningless, it had something empty and inexplicable about it. If pressed to describe it, I would call it a "smile without reason." It seemed to come to his face involuntarily, almost unconsciously, as if only incidentally linked to any of the inner secrets of his business. It occurred to me that, being quite ignorant of the manners of this country, I had perhaps intruded too rudely into his affairs. It would have been only natural, if such were the case, for him to forgive my ignorance and simply refuse to answer. In any event, there had been nothing in the least humorous about my question, nothing that might provoke a smile. I was assuming thus that he would be evasive—when he surprised me no little by launching into a considerably detailed account of his trade.

"I am a little uneasy about revealing such information to outsiders, but since you were good enough to explain the new gun to me, I suppose I owe you as much. I sell my guns to the Kubosama, Lord Matsunaga, Lord Miyoshi, and the bonzes of the Honganji temple, as well as to the Signore of Owari."

As I listened, the source of his laughter dawned on me: he was selling guns to two opposing armies at once—that much was clear even to one as ignorant as I was of the ins and outs of warfare in that land; almost certainly, his little smile was a sign of this duplicity. Yet I was still unsure what, morally, it really signified. Cunning, perhaps—though a merchant, whether selling guns or not, can hardly be considered remarkably sly simply because he seeks to reap the highest possible profits from a transaction. Or the smile might have been a sign that he was troubled by a feeling that he ought to choose one side and cleave to it through thick and thin. Or again, perhaps he smiled out of nervousness, because he was simply too timid to gamble on a victory for either side and was hedging his bets by dealing with both.

It occurred to me then, however, that the smile might have had nothing to do with any consciousness of duplicity. That—or so I reasoned—would at least have been a sign of common decency, a sign that he knew his behavior amounted to treachery, to a breach of faith. It would, in short, have betrayed the discomfort of an uneasy conscience. But here lay the problem. If he had really felt his behavior was evil, then he would, I supposed, have followed moral imperatives to their logical conclusion and ceased selling guns. On the other hand, the fact that he was already selling to both sides must mean that, at least at some point, he had felt it was right to do so; he would have constructed moral criteria by which he could judge himself favorably, and would have defended those criteria with corresponding zeal. To my mind, it had to be one way or the other.

Manifestly, however, Tzuda had no use for my theory or for my sort of moral consistency. While his smile suggested a certain guilt at selling to both camps at once, he went on brazenly doing just that. In short, he had moral standards, and he did not obey them.

What bothered me essentially was that, unlike some of us, he had not troubled to invent new moral standards. At the instant I stabbed my wife and her lover, I had been forced to dismiss the morality that judged my actions as evil, and in its place create a new morality, one whose standards have required my continual attention to maintain, and which I ignore at the peril of my very being. This will to live, to abide by my new moral system, has been the whole point of my existence these past years, and I was sure I could never understand or share Tzuda's indifference.

If Tzuda's manner had been in any sense cold or harsh—more in keeping with what I would expect of one so at peace with his own hypocrisy—we might have found some common ground for communication and I might have learned in time how to respond to this novel lack of morality, as I saw it. But there was no trace of cold calculation in him at all. As the banquet was ending, the same smile appeared on his face again as he asked if I could possibly give him my new Italian gun. Next, he offered to buy it: I might name my own price and he would pay it willingly. When I refused, he proposed various terms, ending finally with the suggestion that I myself go into the gun manufacturing business in Sakai, in which case he would be satisfied with selling the guns on my behalf. Offers came forth one after another until I grew quite annoyed with his importunateness and the unnecessary servility of his manner.

In the end, I refused every offer. I told him that the new guns would be arriving on the Portuguese ships, and suggested he wait until then.

"Even with all I've offered you, you still refuse?" he said, his face reddening. I nodded. He rose, trembling all over.

"You won't let me have it, on any condition?"

"That is what I have said: no." The interpreter rapidly conveyed my meaning to him.

Suddenly, Tzuda's voice rose to a thunderous roar. I did not, of course, understand the words, but I could guess their general import. He was exasperated. He threw back his head, adopting a menacing attitude. His manner was completely changed from a moment before, and he was plainly berating me with all the resources of his vocabulary. Yet oddly enough I felt nothing one way or the other. Although part of my indifference was due to my inability to understand his abuse, I doubt, looking back on it now, whether the words could ever have had their desired effect, for my mind had gone numb. As I left the house, a feeling of futility came over me. But along with the futility I found myself wondering again about the Signore of Owari. My brain was somewhat clouded with saké, but I could not help dwelling a little further on the problem of a man who could be so universally hated.

The long-awaited letter from Father Frois came about four months after this episode, at the beginning of fifteen hundred and seventy-one. We left Sakai immediately. On the road to Kyoto, we saw villages that had been razed and houses from which the smoke was still rising. Refugees streamed along the highways and through the fields, and mounted warriors galloped among the ruins. Everywhere were signs of recent fighting. When night fell, the road was dotted with watch fires, their flames casting flickering shadows on the dark figures of the helmeted warriors the Japanese call *samurai*s.

Checkpoints had been set up along the highway, and soldiers

were toiling to strengthen the forts that punctuated the battle lines. These men, Lorenzo informed us, were under the command of Lord Wada, one of the captains-general who owed fealty to the Gran Signore of Owari, now at court in Kyoto. Father Frois, accompanied by Lorenzo himself, had been granted an audience the previous year with this Signore, who had made various dispensations to help the work of the mission. It was Wada who had acted as intermediary for Father Frois and the Owari Signore on this occasion. And it was he who had provided our escort to the capital, consisting of a young *samurai* and ten soldiers.

As we made our way from Sakai to Kyoto, which was the name by which Miyako, the capital, was known, I often spread out Lorenzo's old, crumpled map in an attempt to identify the various castles, fortresses, towns, and villages we passed and thereby get an idea of the nature of the conflict. Lord Miyoshi, an enemy of the Owari Signore, was advancing from the south, while Asai and Asakura were attacking from the north. The Signore was facing the invading armies in the north, while Wada was pitted against Miyoshi in the south.

"It was God Himself who sent us Lord Wada," Lorenzo assured us as we walked. "He has protected Christians through good times and bad; were it not for Him, our lot at present would be far more difficult than it is." As we passed one of Wada's camps, Lorenzo explained that this lord had not as yet embraced the Christian faith despite his deep sympathies with it.

"How odd," said Organtino, "that he should show us such good will yet not believe." His kind blue eyes glistened, and though it was winter, there were beads of perspiration on his round nose.

"I have heard it said that Lord Wada loves all creatures. The only things he hates are prejudice and selfishness—or so his retainers claim," said Lorenzo.

"If they speak the truth, then he is a man ripe for God to

harvest. We must show such a man our warmest friendship."

While Lorenzo and Organtino were engaged in this exchange, I had been watching several tonsured men being led off by soldiers. "They are bonzes," said Lorenzo, noticing my interest. "Though to all appearances they are holy monks, they are in fact professional soldiers in the employ of the monasteries on Mount Hiei, which have formed an alliance with the armies invading from the north. In the same way, the monks at Ishiyama near Osaka are allied with the armies in the south, and all alike are opposed to the Signore of Owari."

Their robes were splattered with mud, their expressions grim and somber. Their shaved heads were bent, their feet bare and bloodied. The image of these soldier-monks, staggering along bound together by a thick rope, imprinted itself indelibly on my brain.

"What will become of them?" I asked old Lorenzo. He craned his neck forward.

"They will be beheaded," he said. "The Signore will show them absolutely no mercy."

I asked why.

"The Signore is not alone in his lack of affection for these so-called monks," Lorenzo said, scarcely hiding his own contempt for the doomed men. "They care nothing at all for the pursuit of truth but fritter away their time in worthless argument and pointless interpretations of the scriptures they call *sutras*. Their only aim, as all can see, is the satisfaction of their own vanity. But idleness and vanity are far from the worst of their crimes. In theory they are celibate; in practice, however, they are guilty of vile lewdness with the young men who serve them as acolytes, and on occasion they keep concubines as well. Everyone knows them for a band of libertines."

Nor did the diatribe stop there, but continued in a more personal vein as Lorenzo explained how Frois, Vilela, and he himself had at one time been driven from the capital by the treacherous slander of these monks.

We arrived eventually in Kyoto. As we approached the center of the city, the streets grew more crowded; from passers-by we learned that the fighting had temporarily abated, and we could see that many families who had fled to outlying areas were now returning to the city, pulling their possessions behind them. The capital was more spacious than Sakai, but lacked the latter's order and cleanliness. Some of the houses in the streets through which we passed had been burned, others were partially or wholly in ruins, and even those that had escaped damage were dilapidated. Crowds were gathered at the crossroads and people were peddling whatever they had to sell. In the streets children were crying and people wandering aimlessly. I caught a glimpse of a group of old people huddled at the end of an alley, then of a woman with wild, disheveled hair who was apparently searching for someone, perhaps her lost husband. A man wandered past us in a daze, followed closely by a woman who from time to time let out a frantic shriek. Periodically, we saw large crowds of people running off in one direction or another—agitated, we learned, by rumors that the remnants of Lord Miyoshi's army were being rounded up and made prisoner.

When we at last arrived at the church, Father Frois was waiting outside the gate.

"Welcome!" he said, and without further ceremony took Organtino's stocky frame in his arms. He was a man of average height with a sober expression and an unusual vitality. He was constantly on the move: preaching, presiding over meetings, or, in his few moments of leisure, devoting himself to his writing. The epistles he had penned to the secretary-general of the Society of Jesus were famous among the order's members for their detailed observation and subtle powers of expression. Even before arriving in Goa, Organtino knew of the reputation of these letters, along with those written by Father Vilela. Later, while receiving special instruction on the Oriental missions at the San Paolo seminary, he had read copies of Frois's letters over and over again. He had been particularly impressed with the absence of the perfunctory rhetorical flourishes usual in priestly writings. They recorded the bare facts in a style that was, above all else, concise. The language, however, was by no means dry or boring, but conveyed a sense of speed and power, sentences following one another vigorously, recording everything that met the gaze of this keen observer.

While interested, of course, in the picture of the kingdom of Japan painted in those letters, Organtino had been equally if not more intrigued by the character of the painter himself. He cited for my benefit one passage describing a journey from the island of Shimo, or Kyushu, to Yamaguchi and then on to the capital. The description had struck him, he said, for its refusal to exaggerate the difficulties encountered and the total absence of ill will toward the heathen natives—absence, even, of the natural prejudice born of differences in customs and manners.

Frois's reports described the rebellions in Kyushu and Yamaguchi with the precision of language stripped of all but its essentials. Tireless though the eyes of the observer seemed, they were not bent on detecting either good or evil in the actions of others. People simply moved across their field of vision: some believed in God, others did not; some rebelled, others put down rebellions. Cities were born, fortresses fell. Some suffered defeat, others tasted the fleeting intoxication of victory. A day began, ran its course, came to an end. Time passed like flowing water.

Organtino had told me how, as he read the letters in Goa, he had been impressed by the extraordinary spiritual strength of the man who had written such things. During the two years that had passed since then, not a single day had gone by without his envisaging the time when he would meet Frois face to face. And

31

now, Father Frois was standing before him—or, to be more exact, was pacing rapidly from one end of the room to the other as, just as rapidly, he talked:

"You have perhaps already grasped the situation here in the capital. The city is virtually in ruins and has been so for nearly a hundred years. Fighting rages seemingly without end, sundering parents from children and leaving children without parents. Houses are continually being burned, crops are destroyed in the fields, valuables are left to be plundered. In short, the kingdom of Japan is in turmoil. But that is not necessarily a cause for us to despair. As I am sure you are aware, it is precisely when the world is torn by strife that people are most likely to be searching for peace of mind, for something to relieve a life filled with uncertainty. That is why they come knocking at the doors of the church, why their ears are inclined to hear the Word of God."

As he warmed to his subject, Frois was like a veteran army surgeon confronting the bloody and wounded. His eyes seemed to take in the whole of this chaotic country at a glance. His gaze pierced to the heart of the machinations of the state; one felt he could divine what forces were being marshaled in what quarter and who would rise to oppose them. He even seemed to discern the best means of taking advantage of these enmities. I was dumbfounded by his knowledge of the intricacies of politics in this strange and distant land. According to him, the kingdom of Japan was approaching a period of still greater upheaval, drifting inexorably into a vortex of violence whose outcome was quite unpredictable.

"All that may be said with certainty is that a great storm is upon us. The teeth of the land are clenched with the pain of giving birth to a new age." He paused a moment, his hands held with palms outspread.

"And how are we to proceed through such a storm?" asked Organtino. His eyes were opened wide and his good-natured, ruddy face was even more flushed than usual from the excitement of meeting Frois.

"There is only one path open to us," Frois replied, "and that is to accept the patronage of the lord of Owari and his allies. You have no doubt heard from Lorenzo that the Buddhists of this kingdom have slandered us as heretics and are attempting to draw attention from their depravity by launching persecutions against us. They have influence at court and have won as their ally the *governatore* of Kyoto, known as the Kubo-sama. They are seeking the complete interdiction of Christianity."

"Brother Lorenzo has told us of these trials," said Organtino with a flash of anger that you, my friend, would have recognized as peculiar to the peasants of our native land. "Could we not challenge them to debate doctrines?"

"That, I fear, would be ill-advised at present. Once before I faced the priests of the Tendai sect in debate. On that occasion, we met under the auspices of the Gran Signore of Owari, who is a just man; but we could hardly hope for a fair hearing from the *governatore* and his allies, or expect to persuade those who are already determined to suppress our faith. Thus, as I said, our path is clear: the fate of the church must be linked with the fortunes of the Owari Signore.

"It is important to realize that he does not understand Christianity and is unconcerned with the nature of faith. He is in theory a Buddhist, but that is a mere formality. In fact, he does not seem inclined to believe in anything that is not of this world—that he cannot see with his own eyes. He is, in sum, an atheist, as he has told me himself on more than one occasion with a good deal of pride."

"If he feels no sympathy with our beliefs, how are we to rely on his protection for the church?" Organtino's eyes followed Frois as he paced the room. Without breaking stride, the latter answered:

"That is not easy to explain. I can tell you only that he has an unusually curious nature, a keen spirit of inquiry, and—perhaps most important—a thoroughgoing hatred of the Buddhist clergy. That should be enough to work out the principles determining his actions."

Despite this, I noticed that whenever the subject of the Owari Signore arose, his tone became remarkably animated, almost enthusiastic. The lord in question, it seemed, showed unrivaled insight and resolve as a politician. He was also the most tolerant of the lords of the land in dealing with foreign religions. He alone recognized the charitable nature of the padres' work, praising them as superior to the Buddhist bonzes—whose chief activity, he said, was swindling the people. In nearly every conceivable human endeavor—Frois concluded—the Signore was without peer.

I was astounded to find how greatly his estimate of the man differed from that of the good people of Sakai. In them, the Signore had inspired hatred and fear; yet here was an observer who had only the highest praise and admiration for him. I recalled how opinion had been similarly divided concerning the talents and character of Hernán Cortés, and wondered if any man who scaled such heights could ever escape such controversy.

Father Frois reached the far end of the room and wheeled around to face us, talking incessantly. The Owari Signore was about thirty-seven or thirty-eight years of age; he was tall, bony, and agile; his face was narrow and pale; he was clean-shaven. His voice was resonant, his pronunciation clear and precise. He wore his sword day and night, and always kept a lance close at hand. He was an enthusiastic horseman. His manner was harsh and his retainers trembled at his every word, yet he was extremely just by nature and could be moved by the least show of affection. He had almost no interest whatsoever in the opinions of others, seeming to have an almost religious faith in his own ideas and judgments. He was forever full of new schemes, but was far from being the kind of man who, having once lighted on an idea, refuses forever after to alter it. He would in fact discard former principles and opinions without a qualm—even those once regarded as gospel—and did so, indeed, with such regularity that those around him were sometimes inclined to think him merely capricious. Frois maintained, however, that if only one recognized the consistent personality underlying them, one could accept even these bewildering changes. The Signore's most trusted retainers, such as Lord Hashiba, had found favor precisely because they were able to comprehend this aspect of his temperament.

He permitted his generals to drink their saké, and looked the other way when, according to the custom of the land, they forced cups upon one another until they were all dead drunk. But the Signore himself had never been a heavy drinker. He seemed wholly free of vanity and dressed in the simplest manner. In fact, he seemed to care little for what others thought of him or his opinions. He was, in short, supremely self-confident in all matters.

He was constantly hurrying from one encampment to another, from one fortress to the next, attended by no more than twenty or thirty young *samurais*. To see this company dashing past, they said, was to be reminded of a nobleman driving his hounds to the hunt.

In Frois's words, I sensed a deep gratitude for the protection his missionary work had received from this lord. But there seemed to be something else as well. Something about the Signore had the power to capture men's hearts, and though I myself was hardly under its spell at this point, from the time of my arrival in Sakai the subject of the Signore invariably aroused in me an eager curiosity. In just such a way—it strikes me now—I had experienced a strange thrill in bygone days whenever talk turned to the legendary deeds of Hernán Cortés.

Yet even as I listened to Father Frois, I was beginning to wonder just how the Signore planned to extricate himself from his predicament. As I have said, he was, at that moment, surrounded by enemies, of whom those to the north and south were already actively mounting attacks. Here too I recalled my own experience in Nuova Spagna, when the governor Ibarra sent me with a small band of soldiers to quell an insurrection among the Indians. I will not repeat my account of that engagement here, since I have described it in detail in my letter from Malacca. But you will see, I think, that our situation closely resembled the trap into which the Signore had fallen. In short, even as our erstwhile punitive force was cutting through the thick jungles, trying to break through the trap the Indians had set to the north, we were effectively surrounded, being threatened by a still larger band of rebels to the south.

The Signore's situation was much the same: the army pressing him from the south was, I gathered, being supplied with provisions and arms by the provinces to the west, while the army to the north had ensconced itself in the rugged mountains. In concert, they presented the Signore with a number of strategic dilemmas. If he were to move against the north, the army in the south would spring on him from the rear; if he went south, then the north would be free to attack. The brief respite from hostilities which had greeted us on our arrival in Kyoto was due, simply, to Wada's efforts to hold in check the army to the south, and to the fact that a truce was being considered with Asai and Asakura, who led the armies to the north.

Be that as it may, the break in the fighting was seen as particularly fortunate for the work of the mission, and Lorenzo had gathered a good deal of information about the situation. Even so, since it was difficult to judge how long the equilibrium would last, Frois and Organtino were working day and night so as to take full advantage of the relative calm. For the most part, their efforts were directed at repairing the church and reassembling the congregation. Among their flock were many who had lost relatives or whose houses had been burned, so in addition to holding daily masses they struggled to find food, clothing, and shelter for Christians who were homeless or orphaned. Nor did their charity stop there, for they set up a great cauldron on the dry riverbed at a place called Rokujo, and began dispensing rice gruel to all and sundry. I myself, as a rule, accompanied Organtino on those outings.

When Frois at last judged that Organtino had become accustomed to missionary work in the capital, he set out on a trip to Gokinai, as the five provinces surrounding the capital are called. His purpose was to reestablish ties with the isolated groups of Christians who dwelt beyond the bounds of Kyoto. During his absence, Organtino assumed responsibility for writing the reports on the mission, and his lamp would burn far into the night. Never in his life, he told me, had he been more painfully aware of all the people who depended on him.

The hot summer in Kyoto was drawing to a close. An epidemic had broken out to the south of the city, and a rumor was circulating of a whole village having been put to the torch. In the city, people were telling the shocking story of a woman who—unable to find food for her old mother—had forced her to drink saké until she was very drunk, then stabbed the old woman to death and buried the body in the yard. Another rumor current among the citizens of the capital said that a man-eating demon, allegedly from distant Tamba, was appearing from time to time in villages on the northern outskirts. Not a day passed without incidents of arson, robbery, and looting. The city was parched, with only a trickle of water flowing in the dry riverbed. The bodies of those who had collapsed and died in the streets were carted unceremoniously to the outskirts of the town, where scavenger birds squawked with noisy delight over the unattended corpses.

An unpleasant stench hung over everything, and the air was stifling even at night. Troops streamed by, streaked with sweat, and uneasiness hung heavy over all.

One evening, while I was sitting at the side of the church repairing my arquebus, Lorenzo came hurrying around from the front.

"Where's the padre?" His voice was hoarse and his shoulders were heaving. Hearing him, Organtino came running out of the church.

"What is it?" I asked, supporting the old man on my shoulder.

"Last night . . . Wada . . . killed . . . in battle . . . ," he managed to get out, then more or less collapsed.

Organtino went pale. "Wada? Dead? . . ." he said, as if to himself. "Surely it cannot be!"

I myself stood shocked and silent. My first thought, I must confess, was of the unpleasant military consequences of the death of this lord, ally of the Owari Signore. But then I reminded myself that, first and foremost, we had lost a man who by all reports was a good-hearted soul, a man whom the fathers had hoped to claim as a convert in the near future. On a more practical level, his death meant that our activities in Kyoto and the surrounding provinces now exposed us to considerable danger. Though the capital was for the moment relatively peaceful, the inhabitants of the nearby domains of Omi, Ise, and Settsu were in constant ferment. Castles were being attacked and supply routes threatened. The lines of battle, we were told, were constantly shifting. The situation was sufficiently unstable for Lord Wada to have felt it necessary to dispatch a special escort for Father Frois when he left on his tour of the provinces. But beyond the dangers it presented for us, I knew that the death of Wada could have larger consequences: namely, an end to the aid he had been giving the Signore against the hostile armies in the south and east, and the collapse in turn of the fragile equilibrium.

It was deemed absolutely necessary that we contact Father

Frois at once and alert him to this development. Lorenzo went personally to summon several members of the congregation, but we were not able to stir from the church, since by now it was dangerous for a foreigner even to show his face in the streets. The rumor of Wada's death was spreading, and clusters of people were beginning to drift toward the outskirts of the city, fearing that the fighting would soon begin again. Another rumor had it that Miyoshi's army in the south and those of Asai and Asakura in the north were already approaching the vicinity of the capital. As if to give credence to these reports, soldiers were blocking all the principal streets with barricades formed from the uprooted stumps of trees or from logs and sandbags, and mounted warriors were galloping hither and thither with an air of great urgency.

From what Lorenzo had heard while visiting believers in various parts of the city, we too were forced to conclude that the fighting was drawing near. I felt sure at the time, in fact, that my urge to repair my arquebus had been something of a premonition; above all, I felt a personal obligation to protect Organtino from all danger, and I was convinced that the gun might prove necessary in this respect.

Organtino himself was more optimistic than Lorenzo or myself. For one thing, in a few short months he had made startling progress in learning the language, and increasing contact with the people had increased his affection for them. I myself, indeed, had seen very little sign of animosity toward foreigners on the part of the Japanese; if anything they were consumed with curiosity. In a sense, though, it was little more than that; though they would stare at us apparently without malice, they made no attempt to speak with us. In part, of course, this was due to our ignorance of their language, but they also showed a peculiar reserve bordering on timidity. I feel sure that this reserve bespoke no ill will. This was apparent whenever Organtino addressed someone on a street corner—as he had done in Sakai and continued to do in Kyoto. Invariably, such overtures would be met with a look of exceeding courtesy and warmth; once they started talking, in fact, the reticence of most Japanese would soon give way to loquacity.

In the meantime, however, Lorenzo was shaking his head and looking worried; it was plain that the source of his concern was the absence of Father Frois. Late in the afternoon, the old man came into Organtino's room, the graveness of the situation written on his face.

"Padre—I am leaving to see the Signore of Owari at his castle in Gifu. As things stand, we are utterly helpless, and with Lord Wada no longer here to protect us, there is no telling what forms of persecution the Buddhist priests may have in store for us. I am not afraid to die for my faith; but a Christian, as Father Torres often told me, has a duty to fight the good fight to the end. I am going immediately to Gifu to ask for special protection. The Signore knows only Father Frois and myself, and there is no time now to wait for the father's return."

Organtino had no choice but to agree to the old man's proposal. The most he could do to help was to assign some of the young Japanese friars to escort Lorenzo to the court at Gifu. They were to go on horseback along what we hoped might be relatively safe roads. Preparations for the journey were made at once, and they set out under cover of darkness. This was on the eleventh day of September, fifteen hundred and seventy-one.

At the same time, a friar and several members of the congregation rode off in the opposite direction in search of Father Frois. When they had all gone, a quiet fell over the church and we passed a sleepless night thinking of the dangers besetting our companions.

It was in the afternoon of the following day that I spotted smoke rising to the north of the hills they called Higashiyama, or Eastern Hills. The sight reminded me of jungle fires I had seen in Nuova Spagna: black smoke rose like a flag marking the spot where the unseen flames were hottest. Billowing high up into the sky, it swirled there, blocking out the sun as it spread toward the capital. Great blobs of fire hung for a time in the air, then rained down on the city as ash like that from a volcano. White smoke mixed with the black, then, suddenly, the white darkened to yellow. Smoke pillars towered to an astonishing height.

People came running from their homes to stare blankly at the sky. They soon realized that this was no forest fire—so much was apparent from the intensity of the flames and the fact that they showed no sign of moving from one place. Clearly, a town or village was burning. Organtino went out into the street and stopped passers-by to question them.

"What lies beyond the mountain? What is it that's burning?"

But all those he approached were silent, as if in fear, quickly turning their backs and making off. Finally, a fat old man who appeared to be a merchant answered his question, eyeing Organtino all the while with apparent loathing.

"It is probably the Enryaku Temple. The direction is definitely that of Mount Hiei. But why are you asking me? No doubt this is your doing. Once the Buddhists have been disposed of, *your* alms boxes will be stuffed fuller still." He spat out the words and turned away.

When night came, the sky burned so bright that the silhouettes of trees were clearly visible along the ridge from Higashiyama to Kitayama, or Northern Hills. A deep red glow stretched from the horizon high up into the night sky, and through it moved an endless column of smoke. From time to time the sky grew darker and the smoke was more sensed than seen, then suddenly the flames would spew up more brightly than before and the whole scene would be revealed again.

The next morning Lorenzo returned and told us what had happened. It seemed that in the moment prior to the collapse of the precarious military balance, the Signore of Owari had broken through the lines of his enemy and moved to destroy the Buddhists ensconced in the temples of Mount Hiei, who had been giving succor to the bonzes fighting alongside the Signore's enemies in the north.

Throughout the next day, startling reports reached us from the north as smoke continued to rise steadily from the mountain. Piecing together the information, we gathered that the Signore had not only burned all the temples, pagodas, shrines, priests' quarters, universities, and various other buildings crowded on the mountain, but had also had put to death every single one of the several thousand lay and clergy, men and women, who lived there. The horror of this deed could be felt on every street corner in Kyoto; it was as if a bolt of lightning had struck the city. Its inhabitants vanished from sight; even the refugees living on the dry riverbed hid themselves as best they could under the bridges. From time to time, burning flakes continued to rain down on the parched city.

I need not tell you that I too was startled by this development. Yet I was unusual, perhaps, in being not quite sure whether I was saddened by it or rather pleased. One thing was certain: the audacity and swiftness with which the Signore had resolved his dilemma sent a thrill of excitement through me, a thrill all the greater because I understood something of the true nature of the deed. Lorenzo had spoken to me in the past of the superstitious awe with which the Japanese regarded the sacred Buddhist precincts of Mount Hiei. I knew, too, that the great Buddhist university located on the mountain was rivaled only by those of Mount Koya and the Five Zen Monasteries, and that the temples on Mount Hiei—or Hieizan as the Japanese call it—counted among their treasures great works of art, splendid buildings, sacred books, and idols of much significance to their faith. I imagined that the monks who had taken refuge there and the officers of the army sent to attack them had had a tacit understanding that the sacred grounds were not to be touched; and it was the ruthlessness with which that understanding was violated at the Signore's order that had thrown the streets of Kyoto, some leagues distant, into a panic. The people trembled in fear of the retribution that the gods and Buddhas might at any moment rain down upon them.

But there, I knew, lay the genius of the Signore's coup—in doing the unthinkable. It was precisely the failure to act with a similar boldness that sealed our defeat years earlier in the jungles of Nuova Spagna. Our forces decimated by pestilence, fatigue, and hunger, we were unable in the end to mount any attack, whether in the north or the south. The dilemma had called for a solution similar to the Signore's—a swift strike with all our remaining strength to break through the insurgents' lines at one single point—but such resolve had been beyond my commander. Paralyzed with worry over his two-pronged dilemma, he had fretted away any chance of attacking. A stronger man such as the young Lord of Owari might have found the necessary bravery and imagination. . . .

The more I mused on such things, the more I was struck by his boldness; I suppose, in fact, that it was his action then that changed my curiosity about the man into real admiration. From that moment, I was determined that I would meet him.

Following Father Frois's safe return to Kyoto, we gathered to discuss the problems facing us. Frois insisted that we must stay in the capital no matter what happened. The Signore, he assured us, would never abandon the city to his enemies; Wada's death, in fact, had left us with no choice but to follow his earlier plan and seek the Signore's direct patronage. He had come to this conclusion, he said, despite generous offers of protection from Lord Dario, the Christian name taken by the man the Japanese called Takayama, Lord of Settsu; from Lord Joan, that is, Naito of Tamba; and from others of the Christian *daimyos*, or great lords, under

Frois's tutelage. As Organtino noted with admiration, he showed an extraordinarily clear judgment even in the midst of such confusion—a judgment based solely on meticulous observation.

Nor did the older priest's predictions prove misguided. Almost immediately, the Signore's army appeared in the city and, opening the local granaries, began lending rice to the citizens. The people were overjoyed, and the terrified silence that had reigned those several days gave way to celebration in the streets. The men beat the drums they call *taikos* and sang rowdy songs, stripped to the waist as though for a festival even though the season was changing and the evenings were already cool. Old women tottered along weeping aloud for joy and clutching bags of rice, while the young people made merry with flutes and bells. Such jubilation over a little rice was proof that the Signore was a student of human nature and as great a politician as he was a military strategist.

It was around this time that we received a special dispatch from the church in Kyushu saying that Father Cabral had finished his round of inspection on that island and would visit Kyoto and the Gokinai provinces in the near future. I believe I have already indicated that Father Cabral was a man not much to my liking; even the memory of his arrogant ways, in fact, was enough to make me more than a little disgusted. The letter announcing his visit was itself an example of his nature, being filled with the names of *daimyo*s and other powerful men he had baptized in our absence, as if these conversions represented personal accomplishments.

The more I thought about Cabral, the more it seemed that I should go elsewhere before his arrival. There was nowhere else I could go, however, so I contented myself with confiding to Organtino my dislike for his superior. But he merely laughed and refused to take me seriously, saying that even haughtiness such as Cabral's was occasionally of use to the church.

One good that came of Vice-Provincial Cabral's visit was that I was able to meet the Signore sooner than I had expected. This benefit, even so, was preceded by a characteristic piece of unpleasantness. On his arrival in Kyoto, Cabral immediately issued a stern reprimand to Father Frois, taking him to task for what he felt was the meager size of the church building, the over-ly austere decoration of the interior, and the overly commodious accommodations provided, on the other hand, for the Japanese friars. He also, among other things, scolded Organtino for having allowed me to accompany him; no allowance, he said, should be made for my subsistence in the diocesan budget.

Even so, thanks to Organtino's intervention, I was among the company—along with Frois, Organtino, and Lorenzo—that went with Cabral on his visit to Gifu in fifteen hundred and seventy-two. It was, of course, Frois who made all the arrangements, but the guest of honor was the head of the mission to the parish of Japan, Vice-Provincial Cabral. Gifu was a four-day journey from the capital, and much of the way led along the shores of a great freshwater lake. The province was called Omi, and we were told by its inhabitants that the Signore's enemies, Lords Asai and Asakura, were established to the north of the lake.

Gifu was a town of nearly ten thousand souls. To us, accus-tomed as we were to the spaciousness of the capital and the orderliness of Sakai, the place was a veritable Babylon. Markets lined the narrow streets, where all manner of people jostled each other day and night. Noisy throngs filled the open spaces. Men on horseback pushed their way through the congestion, being loudly berated for their efforts. There were merchants hawking their wares, people laughing, people crying out at finding themselves nearly trampled underfoot. Some shouldered heavy bundles, others were seated on the ground eating their meals. Carts were being loaded and unloaded. There were gamblers, merchants, revelers, women, small groups of children, visitors from other provinces, and *ronins*—masterless *samurai*—all marching or shuffling or strolling along to such a clamor that we had to speak loudly into one another's ears to make ourselves heard. We were to be lodged at an inn on the corner of one of these noisy streets, but Cabral said that he could not possibly sleep in such a place, so his quarters were moved to the home of a wealthy man who lived near the castle, while the rest of us stayed at the inn.

The afternoon of the following day we went to the court. The castle was surrounded by a moat which lay at the base of a towering stone wall, along the top of which ran white walls punctured with embrasures through which guns could be fired. The wall itself was topped with beautifully curved tiles. Passing through two large gates, we came to a magnificent building somewhat resembling a theater. A large fruit tree grew at either side of the entrance to the *palazzo*, where we were greeted by upward of thirty soldiers kneeling on mats. Then, accompanied by these retainers, we passed through long, labyrinthine corridors, turning down any number of passageways all lined with sliding doors made, we were told, of cryptomeria wood. Some were closed while others stood open, allowing us to see the handsome chambers within. The doors were decorated with strikingly simple paintings of birds, animals, and plants done in black India ink with perhaps a few touches of green, white, or brown. At last we came to a large hall surrounded by golden doors. The floors were spread with a kind of rush matting, each mat being bound at the edges with beautiful fabric. The room faced a garden with a small pond nestled among rocks and trees, all in accordance with the Japanese custom of fashioning their landscapes to recreate nature in miniature. In the pond, which was lined with white stones, fish were swimming to and fro.

The place reserved for the Signore was a raised dais in the center of the hall. A golden screen had been set up behind it and nearby stood a Chinese desk and a chair. Chairs for Father Cabral and Father Frois were placed facing the Signore, with Lorenzo, who was to act as interpreter, seated in the middle. I sat behind Organtino.

Directly after we had taken our seats, the sliding doors before us parted and a tall man entered surrounded by retainers. We knew without introduction that this was the Signore of Owari. He was very much as Father Frois had described him: the face long and quite pale and the features firm. His eyes were piercing, and his right brow twitched in a most disturbing fashion almost the whole time we were in his presence. Once inside the room, he made a sign to the attendants, who withdrew instantly, almost as if the wave of his arm had been a sorcerer's gesture and they had simply vanished into thin air.

I scrutinized him, intent on finding in his face the features of the bold strategist who had burned the holy monastery, but given his present good spirits it was by no means easy. His dress was wholly without ostentation. He wore simple garments well suited to his simple, direct manner. Strange to say, on the occasion of this audience, this man so widely feared and hated seemed quite cheerful. As he exchanged greetings with Father Frois, the reason came to me why he seemed so favorably disposed toward this particular priest: though Frois was a foreigner, it must have been apparent to the Signore that he too, in his own way, was a man of action and a keen observer.

With the aid of Frois's fluent Japanese and Lorenzo's skillful interpreting, the conversation with the Signore proved most lively. The talk took the form of questions from the Signore to which Frois, Cabral, and occasionally Organtino would make reply. The Signore was clearly delighted with the gifts that Father Frois had chosen. These included: a Portuguese hat lined with velvet, an hourglass, assorted glass vessels, a telescope, a magnifying glass, Cordoba leather, a velvet purse, embroidered handkerchiefs, sweetmeats, fancy foods preserved in sugar, a Portuguese cape, perfume extracted from aloes wood as well as the wood itself, woolens from Flanders, rugs, and various other things besides. Father Frois painstakingly explained each item. He smiled as he said that the hourglass was easier to operate than the alarm clock previously presented to the Signore, and would thus perhaps be of more use. The joke was not lost on us, as he had already told us how the Signore had returned a Venetian alarm clock as being too complicated for him to master to his satisfaction.

While these explanations were proceeding, I began to be apprehensive of a possible indiscretion on the part of our leader, Father Cabral. I am fairly sure that Organtino and Frois, too, shared my anxiety. Cabral was reared, as I have mentioned, in a noble family of Portugal, and was not above boasting of his successes in baptizing the wealthy and powerful. I for one had thought that the interview with the Signore would be gratifying to his pride, but the need for us to meet the Signore and seek his protection must have seemed an intolerable humiliation to such a proud nature. For a while, he contented himself with averting his gaze and hardly replying to the Signore's questions; when he did answer, there was no hint of friendliness in his tone. As the chill became more and more apparent, Organtino, who had made the long voyage out with the Vice-Provincial and was thus familiar with his character, actually began to tremble in a most inappropriate fashion.

"I have heard," offered the Signore at this point, "that Europeans eat a good deal of meat. Is the same true of missionaries?"

At this, Father Cabral threw his head back arrogantly.

"From the tone of your question, I gather you are implying that the eating of meat is of itself an evil. Of course we eat meat!"

It seemed to me—though perhaps it was my fancy—that for a moment a dark shadow crossed the Signore's face. Unconsciously I rose slightly—to be prepared, I suppose, to take whatever action might prove necessary. But the next moment the shadow had passed and the Signore laughed dryly.

"And well you should. In this country it is forbidden for religious men to eat meat, but there is no sense in a law that prohibits holy men from eating what others consume with impunity. At any rate," he added with apparent disgust, "it is common knowledge that our monks eat animal flesh in secret."

Shortly after this exchange, the Signore inquired my occupation. In introducing me, Father Frois had said simply that I was not a member of their religious order but a layman. I gave a brief account of myself and my life as a sailor and explorer, then I expressed admiration for the Signore's daring move in burning the temples on Mount Hiei. At this point, Organtino interrupted to sing my praises as a marksman with the arquebus. He intended perhaps to make amends for Cabral's rudeness; this seemed likely, at least to me, in view of the Signore's well-known interest in the musket.

If this was indeed Organtino's intention, his words had the desired effect. Hardly was the remark out of the father's mouth when the Signore asked me whether I had brought the gun along, and whether I would be willing to demonstrate my skill at once.

I turned to Father Frois, who replied on my behalf that I did not have the gun with me but would be honored to comply with the Signore's request and bring it to the palace the following day. With that, the Signore stood up with a satisfied air and clapped his hands. The retainers reappeared, again as if by magic, and grouped themselves around their lord.

"A meal has been prepared for you in another room, and I have instructed my cooks to include all manner of meats. Please make yourselves at home." He smiled broadly, then turned and left the hall. As he went, Organtino breathed an audible sigh of relief.

The next day, Lorenzo and I again entered the palace. This time, we were shown to a building of simple but solid construction with a wooden floor, opening on a yard that was used as a riding ground. The other sides of the court were bordered by stone walls. The Signore's attendants on this occasion numbered only about ten.

I set up a target at a distance of about fifty paces, and loading my brace of arquebuses fired them in quick succession. Both shots hit the mark. The Signore praised my skill repeatedly, and one of his retainers placed a silver coin on a folding fan and offered it to me. The Signore seemed hesitant, almost self-conscious. The reward, he said, was surely not the appropriate one, but since he had no idea what to give a foreigner, he hoped I would accept it. I can recall the scene most vividly to this day, for I was quite struck by this momentary show of shyness in the midst of his overwhelming curiosity about guns.

I was asked, as I had been in Sakai, to explain the relative advantages and disadvantages of the arquebus and the musket. I said that the musket could hit a target from two or even three hundred paces, but that the gun was long and thick and cumbersome to handle. By contrast, though the arquebus was not much use beyond a distance of fifty paces, the loading of the shot and powder could be accomplished quickly—so quickly in fact that it was possible to have two guns ready to fire in succession. I explained that the principal weakness of a musket company in open-field combat was the defenseless moment between the firing of one round and the loading of the next, and that students of warfare in Europe had been struggling to find a means of protecting the marksmen during that vulnerable period. Usually the task had fallen to the archers, but there were, of course, limits to the effectiveness of bows and arrows. Thus, the plan had been devised of organizing musket companies into two or three files. The first row would fire, then, while it was reloading, the second and third rows would fire in succession, so that by the time the third row had fired, the first would have reloaded and would be ready to fire again. If, in addition to these lines of muskets, one could deploy a company armed with arquebuses, it would quite likely be possible to reduce the enemy's numbers by fully half by the time the lines joined battle. In France, I said, both mounted and infantry troops had been armed and reorganized along these lines.

As I was giving this summary of European battle tactics, the Signore constantly interrupted with questions about the lie of the land in the type of warfare I was describing, or the types of battle array and the length of time required to deploy each, the pros and cons of columns, methods of coordinating the movements of one unit with another, ways of subdividing units, and tactics for defending one's troops against an enemy armed with guns of its own. He also had questions about the different types of fortress, the uses of a vanguard, strategies against artillery, and numerous other topics. Finally, he asked whether I had shown the gun to anyone else. I explained in some detail what had transpired in Sakai, whereupon he instantly issued an order to one of his attendants. He then asked whether I would consider selling, or at least lending him, an arquebus. I replied that I had naturally come with the intention of offering my guns to the Signore.

Ten days later I was again called to the palace. To my surprise, I was shown several new arquebuses that had been made in the brief period since my previous visit. I picked up one of them and weighed it in my hand. It was all but impossible to detect a difference between the new gun and my own, and I communicated my astonishment to the Signore.

"I would like you to test the workmanship," said the Signore. The pale skin of his brow was twitching and his eyes shone.

I took one of the guns and fired at the target, but the barrel was warped and the gun useless. The base of the firing mechanism in the next was bent and the gun would not fire at all. In the end, only two of the new guns were serviceable, but this still seemed to me ample evidence of the advanced state of gunsmithing in the

Signore's kingdom. Lorenzo told me shortly thereafter that the Signore had reorganized his musket companies and was putting them through rigorous training—apparently in the maneuvers I had suggested.

I realized around this time that Lorenzo was not only my informant in most matters having to do with this kingdom, but also my only voice. And though I had advanced to the point where I could manage a simple exchange in Japanese, the old friar's return to Kyoto left me a virtual mute. The situation troubled me, and I began to think that I should make a serious study of the language. Most of all, I will admit, I wanted to speak with the Signore without an interpreter, to make firsthand contact with the multitude of thoughts that seemed to be racing through his mind.

I was still in Gifu, engaged in a diligent study of the Japanese tongue, when new tremors began to shake the delicate balance newly restored by the burning of the holy monastery. The army of Lord Shingen to the east began to move against the Signore, and the armies to the north and south, acting in concert, began to apply pressure of their own. At the same time, the *governatore* of Kyoto, who up to this point had given only secret support to the Signore's enemies, suddenly began to demonstrate open hostility toward the Signore.

A strong streak of anxiety became apparent in the prevailing clamor at Gifu. Whole families were to be seen carting off their possessions, and the cries of the merchants grew shriller, their prices lower, as they tried to dispose of their stock quickly. Troops were leaving daily for battle, and a rumor spread that Shingen's army was approaching from the east to burn Gifu in revenge for the Signore's destruction of the holy mountain. His force was said to number twenty or even thirty thousand men— some said as many as fifty thousand. It was as if a sinister tide were lapping at the city's shores, threatening to engulf it. Remaining at court, I began instructing a company of young soldiers in marksmanship, all the while anxiously watching the progress of the war, wondering how the Signore would extricate himself from these new dangers.

Insurrections broke out in several provinces, as rebels took advantage of the Signore's difficulties to press their causes. The immediate problem, however, remained the army of Lord Shingen. Twenty or thirty thousand strong, it was approaching from the east like a dagger jabbing at the Signore's heart, and action against it was increasingly imperative. Every day, impatiently, I drilled the handful of men who were to form my arquebus corps, but they had yet to master the techniques of loading and firing. I had learned during my difficult days in Nuova Spagna that if these were to be of any use face to face with the enemy, they must be practiced until they became more or less reflex actions. But this took time—a good deal of time.

Surveying the Signore's dilemma from my admittedly limited perspective, I was most concerned lest the *governatore* of Kyoto take advantage of the Signore's difficulties with Shingen in the east to lead the northern army in an attack from the rear. In open warfare such as would be fought on the plains of the provinces of Mino and Owari, victory nearly always fell, I knew, to the larger force. It was not feasible thus for the Signore to tackle the twenty or thirty thousand men in the east with only a portion of his forces. During the day, I would attempt to guess what he might decide to do; at night, I would climb the watchtower and stare off eastward into the darkness, imagining the vast army advancing on us unseen. Once, a shooting star fell through the night sky, and I had a disturbing feeling that the star was the Signore's approaching fate. . . .

One morning, going out into the courtyard of the castle, I discovered that the remaining forces had left for battle while I slept. I also learned that they had not gone east, but were headed in the least expected direction: southwest toward Kyoto. The audacity of this gambit left me breathless and uncomprehending. It was true that the Kubo-sama was in Kyoto directing the most recent attempts to surround the Signore, but the Signore's enemies could hardly have anticipated that he would ignore Shingen's forces in the east and come instead to Kyoto, where he would be utterly trapped between the northern and southern armies. Thus the surprise was complete when the Signore appeared in the capital and surrounded the governor's palace.

I gathered what information I could from secondhand accounts of the reports that came at frequent intervals from Kyoto. I knew already that Organtino and Lorenzo had taken refuge in Saga, but Father Frois had insisted on staying in Kyoto, and I could not discover what had become of him after the battle began. It seemed that confusion in the capital was again reaching a peak. Once more, as the Signore's troops entered the city, people began to haul their possessions off to outlying villages. There were tales of women running shrieking through the streets, and of others abandoning their children to flee alone. More official messages suggested that the Signore was negotiating a truce with the Kubo-sama, but with the ring drawing ever tighter around the former, it was difficult to imagine that the latter would be inclined to consider his overtures. For four days, the Signore waited patiently while the *governatore* remained locked in his palace, giving no sign one way or the other.

The first messenger to arrive in Gifu on the fifth day reported that the Signore had suddenly ordered seven of his generals to raze over ninety towns and hamlets in the area surrounding Kyoto. The following day, it was reported that the district known as Kamigyo, where the mansions of the great nobles were located, had been burned at the Signore's bidding. It was the day after this great conflagration that the Kubo-sama agreed to the Signore's proposal.

Everyone was aware, however, that this truce was at best a temporary measure, since the Kubo-sama continued to anticipate attacks by his allies to the north and south. His agreement with the Signore was a way of buying time; once the forces to the south had reached the outskirts of the city, he slipped out of his palace and again unfurled his battle colors, this time as one flank of the southern army. Meanwhile, the army to the north was also about to enter the city. To make matters worse, Shingen's army continued to inch toward Gifu in the east. It seemed that the Signore's luck was exhausted.

One day, however, just when things were at their blackest, events took a most improbable turn. Without warning, the forces at the Signore's back—the aforementioned army of Lord Shingen—broke off their attack and withdrew peacefully from the border of the province like a retreating tide. A few days later a spy reported that Lord Takeda Shingen, the commander, had suddenly taken ill and died. His army, in secret mourning, was silently marching back the way it had come.

It was an absolutely improbable stroke of good fortune. Even the extraordinary Cortés never had such luck. Darkness had suddenly turned to light; against all expectations, the Signore had been released from the noose. Nor was he one to miss this brief, unlooked-for opportunity. Taking personal command of the main body of his forces, he headed for the northern shore of the great lake and immediately launched an attack against his enemies in that quarter.

This offensive was launched early in the summer; before autumn was upon us, the fortresses of Asai and Asakura were in flames and their armies destroyed. By the time the leaves began to fall in the mountains of Echizen and Omi—the northern provinces held by the enemy lords—the Signore's troops were pursuing the last fugitive *samurai*s of the defeated armies from village to village in the distant north.

During the new year celebrations, fifteen hundred and

seventy-four, I had occasion to attend for the first time one of the special banquets which the people of this kingdom hold at that time of year. The interior of the court had been carefully cleaned, the gates were decorated with pine boughs, and simple decorations made of heavy cord and folded white paper hung over the entrances. From early morning, the *daimyos* and generals began gathering at court to offer their congratulations for the new year. According to their rank and station, they were shown to one or the other of the numerous rooms which had been readied for the serving of saké and comestibles of great variety and abundance. I joined them in making a congratulatory visit, offering greetings to the Signore and conveying messages from Father Frois and Organtino, along with sweetmeats and glass vessels. The Signore ordered my *çacazuqui*, or wine cup, filled and urged me to drink.

Later, I heard a rumor that at that evening's banquet the Signore had adorned the table with something more than food and drink. He had, it was said, set out the skulls of Asai and Asakura—who had been put to the sword after their defeat— lacquered black, with flecks of gold. I already knew as a fact that the forces sent to the north had been instructed to put to death every last man, from generals down to the lowliest foot soldier. But that had apparently been insufficient: the heads of these unhappy lords had indeed, it seemed, been separated from their bodies and put on show in the manner related: an act well calculated to display both the cruelty and the thoroughness of its author.

One could see the shadow of terror on the faces of those who whispered this rumor. Nor were the whispers confined to the common folk; nobles of my acquaintance—among them Lords Sakuma and Araki, both intimates of Frois—asked me if I did not think that the Signore's brutality had at last exceeded all measure. Did I, coming from a Christian country, not disapprove of such utter mercilessness? They had plainly been shocked at the burning of Mount Hiei, and again at the razing of the ninety villages around Kyoto. But the expedition to exterminate the northern army seemed to have affected them more deeply still. Hearing one of them murmur that such brutality was "utterly inhuman," I suddenly recalled the very first rumors I had heard of the Signore while I was still in Sakai.

I will not for a moment try to convince you, my friend, that the Signore's military strategy was anything but brutal. Yet I was too well acquainted with another side of the man to dismiss him simply as a cruel tyrant. As I have tried to suggest, he also possessed a childlike shyness and frank curiosity. He had an indomitable spirit of inquiry, and at times his attitude was genuinely cheerful. Above all, he was an acutely sensitive man. Though this may sound odd, I was somehow convinced that the bloody massacre had not, at the very least, been motivated by self-will or petty personal enmity. It is true that almost to a man the citizens of this kingdom, from great lords to humble peasants, trembled in the Signore's presence. He was in some ways more like an absolute monarch. Yet the term as applied to him should suggest, not powerful, brutal kings such as those of Persia or Assyria, but, rather, coolly calculating men of the caliber of Cosimo de' Medici.

He was always, in fact, inclined to listen to the counsels of reason. I have seen, for example, his unhesitating willingness to abandon even the most cherished notion or scheme when confronted with a more reasonable proposition. How different this was from my foolish commander in Nuova Spagna, who would stubbornly persist in the most capricious scheme! That wretched old man had lost the ability to recognize the truth; or perhaps he saw his mistakes but was too proud, too bent on preserving his reputation, to admit them. Either way, my personal experience of other men with pretensions to greatness only reinforced my preference for the Signore's earnest attempts to pursue the rational path regardless of the repercussions on his reputation. He had made, as I suppose is apparent, a very deep impression upon me.

From the moment I saw the flames rising above the holy mountain, turning night into day, I had a sense that the real man was quite different from the one who so terrified those about me. My feelings here were no doubt different even from Organtino's. But the more I met the Signore, the more my ability to speak Japanese improved, the more I was convinced that those feelings were correct. In the fact that he believed in neither the gods nor the Buddhas, trusting only in what his eyes could see, I saw proof that he sought the rational approach in all things. In that sense, he was more a realist than Carlo V, and more thoroughgoing— more consistent even—than Alphonso of Ferrara, who had haggled so endlessly with Louis XII and Henry VIII. Nor was his disdain for religions of the common kind. Men such as my own father also professed not to believe in God, but went to worship nonetheless because, they said, it would be folly to provoke the church. The Signore's convictions were more single-hearted. He had, in fact, made a religion of the search for truth through rational inquiry, and he practiced that religion with utter sincerity. His state of mind would have been completely beyond the comprehension of my father and those other thoughtless epicureans who, while professing to put their faith in the actual world, in fact worshipped only a vague *status quo*. A careless observer might have confused their beliefs with the convictions of the Signore, but an examination of whither their fancies led them in practice will make the difference apparent. In them, the notion that the only reality was the present world caused them to see wine, women, and a comfortable life as the supreme good; these were the things that gave their lives meaning, and anything that threatened to deprive them of these benefits threw them into a panic. The vulgarity in the faces of such men cannot be concealed.

The Signore, however, was not attached to the material world, but to the various manifestations of reason in that world. It was almost as though he felt that, by always acting according to reason, he maintained a kind of freedom, much as the weathercock is firmly attached to a single point only so that it may turn more readily in the direction of the wind.

In those days, it seemed to me, the Signore must have kept in his head a kind of diagram of the military situation, one showing all the forces pressing in around him, rather like a diagram of a chess board where checkmate is threatening. In all his strategies, his one concern was skillfully to handle those interacting forces in all their various and constantly shifting combinations. Each detail was considered in terms of its effect on the final resolution. My arquebus for instance was doubtless, for him, a factor of considerable potential importance, one to be assigned a certain value in his equation, thus enabling him to calculate with almost mathematical exactness the force needed to counter an enemy of a given strength when it was taken into account.

He had only one military and political principle: to win by power in a world of power. Having laid down this principle, he acted on it with every means at his disposal, regardless of such considerations as personal safety. His pages were fond of telling how, even when defeated in battle, he seemed quite calm, almost as if he viewed his own possible demise as just another move in the power contest. He was not one to shed tears of chagrin, and seemed an utter stranger to regret. A defeat meant simply that, in a meeting between a stronger and a weaker force, one's own had been the weaker; and for the Signore, after suffering defeat, the only possible course of action was to bolster the strength of the inferior force. I imagined that the look of composure on the Signore's face was a feature common to men of his sort—men such as Cortés or Vespucci (whom my father had known in Florence)—who constantly confronted crises and who managed to overcome them with reason as their chief weapon.

In this sense, I think it could be said that even the cruelest of the Signore's deeds—the burning of the sacred mountain and the slaughter of its inhabitants, or the annihilation of the northern army and the display of the heads of its commanders—represented nothing but clearsighted obedience to his principle: nullify the opposing force, eliminate all opposition. For the Signore, only single-hearted devotion to that principle gave any meaning to human existence; only by remaining true to this conviction could one preserve a sense of dignity as a human being.

The Signore's utter isolation in his own court was due in part to differences of opinion with his own commanders, who would come to him on occasion to ask that he spare the lives of those who had sued for peace, or begged for mercy, or simply surrendered. In not a few instances, the prisoner in question was a relative or acquaintance of the commander who came to urge clemency; yet never once did the Signore break with his principle. He was fond of comparing his conviction to a building built up stone by stone on firm foundations. If even a single stone were badly laid—if, just once, one went against the principle—the whole would crumble in a heap.

The Signore was not intent on victory above all else. It was simply that he saw victory as the natural consequence of rational action, and rational action was the only thing that had meaning for him. In the same way, I feel, his hatred of the Buddhist priesthood derived not from a whim or any personal enmity, but from his love of reason. Even his friendship for us was, perhaps, less a matter of personal feeling than of his interest in guns and strategies, in the techniques of building and sailing a caravel, in telescopes, and in the various other products of the natural sciences. This suspicion was reinforced one day when he was questioning me about the system of education in Europe. He listened politely enough while I spoke of the universities at

Padua, Bologna, Paris, Salamanca, Rome, Ferrara, and Cracow, but when I turned to the study of the natural sciences, he leaned forward eagerly and questioned me in great detail. When we had done, he folded his arms, fixed his gaze on an invisible spot on the floor, and for a time was totally lost in thought.

Presently, I asked him what one studied at Japanese universities. "Nothing"—he answered as if trying to spit out some foul object—"but the art of translating from one of the world's most useless languages. Even so, the men thus engaged pretend that it is noble work for a human being." Later, I learned that Japanese universities, unlike their counterparts in Europe, were devoted solely to the training of—in this case, Buddhist—priests, so the Signore's remarks must have referred to the exegesis of their holy scriptures, which was the main task of the students.

During that year, I was summoned to the court several times, and my advice was sought on the organization of the musket companies. I continued drilling my arquebus corps in the three-rank method of firing, as well as in the deployment of this formation and the proper manner of marshaling the troops afterward. We did this against the time when we would first join the full army in joint maneuvers. These exercises were held on the wide plain that opened to the south of Gifu, and had as their chief aim the coordination of strategies among the gun companies, archers, and lancers. The basic strategy was this: a frontal attack by the three-ranked musket companies, the establishment of an abatis to hinder the enemy's mounted troops, a temporary retreat to draw the enemy forward, then an attack from both flanks by the mounted lance corps.

It was early on the morning of the twenty-third day of June, fifteen hundred and seventy-four, that a messenger came to summon me to the Signore's encampment. In the pale glow before dawn, I could just make out the dark forms of soldiers as, row after row, they moved by me. They jostled past, almost touching me, the smell of their sweat reminding me of a herd of wild beasts. A short distance away, columns of mounted soldiers galloped along a dike. There were no torches. The march was being accomplished in the half-light and in total silence. Looking up at the North Star, I noted that the army was headed south.

The defeat of the northern army had meant at least a temporary lessening of the danger from that direction, and the Kubosama had been defeated and banished from Kyoto. The death of Shingen had improved conditions in the east, so there remained only Lord Miyoshi (who was apparently contemplating an attack from the south of Kyoto) and the forces allied with him—in particular, Mori in the west, who was supplying arms and provisions.

Around this time, however, I began to realize that there was a "shadow partner" to the Signore's enemies, and that this partner was, in fact, the Buddhist sect known as Ikko. I recalled the grim, fear-twisted faces of the monk-soldiers I had seen the day Organtino and I had first arrived in Kyoto. The Ikko monks, it seemed, with the exception of those who guarded their principal fortress at Ishiyama in Osaka, were engaged in a kind of guerrilla warfare, setting up rudimentary strongholds and resisting in any way they could. If, however, they saw that the opposition was likely to be stiff, they would suddenly and completely disband, retreat, and vanish into the surrounding villages like water poured on sand. No matter how diligently they were pursued, it was impossible to learn where they had gone. Then, once the search had ended, a handful of these monks would reappear as if by magic, and band together. These few would link up with another small band, and in no time at all a great army was again being formed. Moreover, these groups were most unpredictable in their activities, now joining with the main army to swell its ranks, now splitting off to make endless surprise attacks wherever the Signore might be weakest. The damage thus inflicted was in no sense negligible; indeed, now that the immediate danger from the encircling armies had somewhat diminished, this stubborn and widespread resistance from the Buddhists, which had hitherto been masked by the movements of greater enemies, suddenly seemed all the more of a challenge. Joining the army heading south, I was promptly informed that we were going to attack Nagashima, a Buddhist stronghold allied with Ishiyama in Osaka.

Dawn had broken by the time I reached the Signore's camp, and hundreds of banners were fluttering in the cool breeze of early summer. The army had been deployed in long, deep ranks surrounding the fortresses of Nagashima, which were situated on the delta plain at the mouth of a large river. As it joined the sea, the river divided into several streams separated by swampy flats. Thick clusters of reeds grew along its banks, and beyond the reeds lay marshy expanses of land. In the distance, the summer sky was reflected on the surface of pools of water collected between sandbanks.

Here at Nagashima the forces of Buddhist insurrection had twice before used the delta and the marshes to repulse the Signore's army. The place gave great advantage to the defender; the reeds conferred a cloak of invisibility from behind which the rebels could make surprise attacks, then, when pressed, vanish again almost instantly. For a large invading army with relatively inflexible battle formations, however, the reeds were an impassable obstacle. Not only was the line constantly being disrupted by sudden raids, but the numerous small streams made coordinated activity by a large body difficult. Taking full advantage of these natural defenses, the monks at Nagashima had constructed four stockades around the main fortress, and from these they launched their sallies.

In this latest attempt to dislodge the rebels, the central army under the Signore's command was advancing from the north to surround the fortresses. Before the sun was quite up, it appeared that the foremost ranks had encountered the enemy's advance guard, for the reeds in the distance were seen to be disturbed, and a war cry went up. From the east came the army under the command of the Signore's eldest son, while from the west the forces of Lords Sakuma and Shibata attempted to cross the streams and begin their assault. The defense was quite skillful, the insurgents maneuvering small boats from bank to bank, holding their lances at the ready to repel the soldiers trying to come ashore. This time, however, the Signore's army was prepared for skirmishes with these smaller, more mobile forces. The plans for battle had been conceived so that the lines could accommodate very rapid advances and retreats, and by such means the enemy's small bands were continually surrounded and wiped out. Then, when the general advance had reached the vast reed thickets, the musket companies were called. The long ranks of marksmen spread out facing the thickets, then all fired at once, raining shot on the unseen enemy amidst the reeds. The balls found their marks; several dozen men who had been waiting in ambush tumbled from their hiding places, spurting blood.

Unlike the previous unsuccessful attempts, this attack on Nagashima gave the Buddhists no opportunity to mount a counterattack. Like a heavy chain drawn in an ever-tighter circle, the lines of battle contracted steadily toward the center of the delta. Houses on several of the outlying islands were already in flames. Not that the advance was without cost. As night fell, the rebels seemed to rally, and heavy casualties were suffered on the Signore's side as well.

It was only after victory in these first skirmishes had been assured, and preparations made for besieging the strongholds, that the Signore, late at night, summoned his navy. I had slept on the battlefield not far from the Signore's camp, and woke that morning to see the great ring of ships, large and small, pressing into the delta. The sight of this fleet bristling with countless glittering spears was breathtaking; and I suddenly realized that the whole of the Signore's might was being thrown into the attack.

With the first light of day, the sailors of this great force rent the heavens with a terrible battle cry and began their onslaught. First, the ships bearing musket companies were maneuvered alongside the banks of the delta where the enemy lines had taken up their positions. A first round was fired, then, before the smoke had cleared, another. Amidst the clouds of smoke, the rear ranks of the Buddhist soldiers could be seen leaping forward over the bloody bodies of the fallen front line. But in the next instant the guns fired again with a deafening roar. Half the monks fell then, as those who remained hesitated, a fourth round was fired. Wave upon wave of boats pushed up the river in a cloud of spray, attacking the enemy lines as they began to waver. Suddenly, the line gave in one spot, and at once the whole began to crumble. The Signore's forces broke through in several places; a route ashore had been established. With the lines breached and the Signore's troops landing, pitched battles broke out across the delta. Soon, the Buddhists were in general retreat into their fortresses, fighting to protect their rear as they fled.

These fortresses had been erected on the delta plain to form a line of defense around the main stronghold of Nagashima. Each was provided with high earthern embankments topped with various fortifications: wooden fences, turrets, and barricades made from stumps of trees with the roots turned outward to confound attackers. As the Signore's troops approached, showers of sharp arrows rained down from these walls without cease.

When the slaughter on the plain was complete, the musket companies were deployed in three ranks around one of the fortresses, with the archers at ready behind them and the lance bearers held back in the rear. Thus the siege was laid, and there was no chance of escape for the rebels. A message from the Signore came to the captains at the front and was read aloud to the whole army. No doubt, it said, there were women and children in the fortresses in addition to the rebels themselves, but absolutely no mercy was to be shown to anyone. The instructions were explicit: the very reeds were to be parted to the roots to find any who might try to hide; and all, without exception, were to be put to death. If an arm had been hewn from a body, the other was to be cut off as well. Every staring eye in every corpse was to be gouged out. Every object that was Nagashima, every stick and stone, must be utterly destroyed, burned, annihilated.

After the decree was read, a peculiar silence fell over the army for a moment. But then, suddenly, a tremendous battle cry echoed over the delta. The attack on the first fortress had begun. The front rank of musketeers fired, a cloud of dust rose above the earthen fortifications, and holes appeared at several places along the wooden wall. The second row fired, and the bodies of soldiers could be seen lurching from the watchtowers and falling to earth in a graceful arc. The third file fired, then the archers loosed a cloud of flaming arrows. Here and there the walls began to burn, and black smoke wreathed the fortress. Forms emerged from the smoke and attempted to break off the flaming arrows, but the first rank of marksmen fired again. A deafening report rumbled ominously across the plain. Suddenly, the walls burst asunder and dozens of bodies fell in a heap on the embankment. At this, the lancers charged into the breached defenses, and the whole army followed like a great river breaking through a dam.

A young peasant who had leaped down from the tower to shore up the line had his skull promptly cleft and fell vomiting blood. Nearby, a monk wielding a long sword had managed to cut down several of the invaders before a soldier stabbed him with a lance. As he stumbled forward, a second soldier split open his shaved head and a great spray of blood showered the lancer. Inside the fortress, a young woman fell down before a soldier crying for mercy, but he plunged his spear in her back, impaling her like a writing insect on a pin. Yet still the defenders offered stubborn resistance, and there were many dead and wounded among the attackers as well. It was nearly nightfall before this first fortress had been thoroughly sacked.

Throughout the night, orders to the Signore's various armies came at intervals from his camp. A strict vigil was to be kept to prevent any communication between the remaining fortresses and to guard against surprise attacks. The watch fires flickered in the breeze from the sea.

The summer night, however, was brief. When dawn broke, it seemed that the army was arrayed for the siege just as before— with the single difference that one of the fortresses now lay in ruins. The troops were hushed and tense. The occasional arrow or jeering cry from one of the fortresses elicited no response from the men laying siege. An ominous silence hung over the delta. Not a reed stirred. The noises from within the walls ceased, and the only sound was the rippling of waves on the river or the occasional shrill cry of a warbler darting through the thicket in search of its nest.

The navy was still at anchor in the mouth of the river, but it too was silent. Heaven and earth were strangely still; alone, the summer sun moved slowly across the sky. In the afternoon, clouds appeared from the direction of Gifu and turned the sky a dazzling white.

The wind stirred presently, but inside the fortresses all was still as death. The Signore had begun a blockade to starve out the resisters. Spies had reported that the attack had taken the defenders of Nagashima by surprise; there was, at most, no more than a month's supply of food in the fortresses. The Signore gave orders that the siege should continue as long as necessary. Under no circumstances were supplies to be allowed to slip through. Reports arriving from Kyoto and elsewhere concerning the situation throughout the rest of the land convinced the Signore that there would be sufficient time to finish the task in hand before his attention was demanded elsewhere.

Days passed, late summer came. The wind would arise in the evening and thunder rumble in the distance. Occasionally, black clouds would descend from the north and a storm would roll across the delta. One night of heavy rain, a flash of blue-white lightning revealed a dark figure to a soldier out on patrol. He said later that he thought it was only the shadow of reeds bending in the driving rain, but he was waiting for the next flash of lightning when a sharp blade pierced him in the back and he lost consciousness.

The next moment, a whistle sounded and a great mass of figures loomed up. The whistle had signaled a desperate exodus from one of the remaining fortresses. In the midst of the storm, a fierce battle was joined. As alarms sounded in the Signore's camp his soldiers scrambled after the insurgents, who were soon in full flight through the darkness. In the end, none of them reached safety, and the carnage was complete. The fields were littered with bodies—an old man pierced through the back by a heavy spear, a woman split nearly in two at the shoulders, children trampled underfoot, a monk cut utterly to shreds. The corpses were starved and emaciated, as though they had already become skeletons. The next morning, a thousand bodies were counted: men, women, and children, a lifeless mass washed by the torrential rain.

In the three fortresses that continued to resist, the situation was apparently much the same. Many times emissaries emerged to discuss surrender, but on each occasion they were seized, nailed to crosses, and set out for the remaining occupants to ponder. Summer ended and the wind in the reeds made a mournful, dry rustling, but the siege continued. The weather began to change. Lines of high, fleecy clouds streamed in from the sea. At night the air was cool and insects called from among the grasses as the moon shone overhead.

The siege was now more than three months old, and it was learned that fully half the occupants of the fortresses were already dead of starvation. Yet still there was no sign that the survivors would try to force their way out. Among the Signore's commanders there was a feeling that the time was fast approaching when the battle of Nagashima would have to be decided by some final, decisive action, particularly in the light of recent reports that the Takeda army, which had temporarily withdrawn to the east, was once again on the move under the command of the late Shingen's son.

Such was the situation on the day when an aide from the Signore's camp suddenly ran out toward the castle and fired a message tied to an arrow up and over the wall. With this, the Signore's entire army began to withdraw. The final application for surrender had been accepted, and the wave of joy and relief within the fortresses was palpable in the air. The army arrayed on the delta boarded the ships, which immediately made their way out of the mouth of the river. Less than half an hour after the last companies had embarked, the gate of the main fortress opened like a dam bursting, and men and women poured out. In a great swarm like locusts, they hurried down to the water and boarded small boats hoping to reach the opposite shore and the safety of the mainland. But just as this chaotic exit was subsiding into orderly flight, a great and terrible roar sounded from the guns of the ships. Spray rose around the boats of the fleeing Buddhists. A number of people tumbled into the river, while many more slumped over in the boats.

Those still standing on the delta outside the fortress scattered at the sound of the shots, stumbling over the bodies of those who had already fallen. Taking careful aim, the three lines of musketeers fired in succession. Spray rose in clouds and bodies fell heaped one on the other. The people in the boats plunged into the water, and those on land similarly scrambled to seek whatever protection the river could provide.

"We are betrayed! Betrayed!" they cried as they threw themselves in the stream. In the space of a minute, the water was roiling with people clinging to one another in knots or struggling to reach the far bank. Some were instantly swept away in the fast current, others were swallowed by whirlpools, but the stronger swimmers, some oozing blood from their wounds, continued to fight their way across, thrashing along like starving rats swarming into a pond. From time to time as they swam, one or the other of them would swallow a great gulp of water and slip beneath the surface, only to bob up again after being dragged some way downstream by the current.

Just as the ablest swimmers were reaching the middle of the stream, the boats of the Signore's navy pulled even with them. The half-starved rebels, lacking the strength to resist the current, drifted in among the boats like so much black seaweed. Those who continued to swim were skewered through the back with long spears, and even the bodies of those who were apparently dead were slashed with swords. Before our eyes, the river ran red, and an unmistakable smell of blood spread over the delta. Some of the women and old people who were swimming more slowly made straight for the boats, maddened by the fear of drowning, and grasped the rails, screaming and pleading for mercy. The soldiers merely prodded them off with lances to drown in the current or, if any clung fast, drew their swords to lop off the hands at the wrist. Soon ten or twenty such hands, stiff and pale as if carved from stone, adorned the rail of every boat in the river.

At the sight of their women and old people dying in such a fashion, the last defenders who had remained in the main fortress drew their swords, and pouring forth fell upon the fleet. Laying hold of the boats, they slew many of the Signore's men. This counterattack, coming like a sudden squall, threw the ranks into confusion. For a moment, the whole army seemed poised for flight. The rebels charged, then broke through the stout lines of the siege, escaping to the opposite shore.

Night was falling by the time the last women, children, and invalids left behind in the castle had been beheaded. In the half-light, the castle itself was burning with an appalling brightness. The defenders of the two remaining garrisons, witnessing the end of the main fortress, had apparently shut their gates the more tightly, determined to resist while they could. With the main stronghold gone, however, they could only watch helplessly as the Signore's men piled up mountains of dried brush and bundles of straw around their walls. Presently, these two fortresses were put to the torch in turn. It was said that more than ten thousand men and women were reduced to ash that day.

By October, the rebellion of the Buddhist monks at Nagashima had been completely crushed. With the exception of seven or eight hundred priests and peasants who had managed to escape in a final flight, the occupants were slaughtered to the last soul. Just as when the sacred temples were burned on the mountain, here, too, resistance was utterly crushed.

III

My friend, a royal court, be it in Florence or Milan or Lisbon, is a lonely place; it did not take me long to realize that the court at Gifu was no exception. To be sure, the Signore was constantly surrounded by thirty or more attendants, and on occasion would engage some among them in friendly conversation. There were banquets, too, and tea ceremonies to relieve his solitude, and he was fond of falconing. When he went hunting, it was generally a festive occasion with the ladies of the court allowed to accompany the party. More commonly, however, he found his diversion on the training grounds of the gun companies or cavalry.

Though he was not, thus, without companionship and recreation, the Signore gave the impression, even when surrounded by many people, of being somehow isolated, as though wrapped in chill air or cut off by an invisible wall. When he passed along a corridor, his gaze fixed on some unseen point, his pale brow twitching, it was as if he left a shadow in his wake. Nor were these impressions mine alone. Among the men who attended this great lord were some whose expressions would go painfully tense at the slightest word from him, and others, even, whose cheeks twitched or whose heads bobbed uncontrollably on their necks. I myself can bear witness that not only his humbler attendants—in whom, indeed, it was fitting enough behavior—but generals and *daimyo*s also made it a habit, in coming before the Signore, to approach no nearer than an antechamber several yards distant from his person. I might add, too, that it was no secret that the Signore took frequent advantage of the awe in which he was held; seeing him, I felt that his tall, pale-faced figure at such moments embodied— perhaps quite intentionally—just that brutality and cruelty that I had heard rumored since my arrival in Sakai. Even so, considering that there were many old, established retainers who were in contact with the Signore day in, day out, it did seem unnatural that he should emanate such a consistently sinister, chilly atmosphere.

From the time I first came to Gifu, I often heard speculation as to why the Signore should be on such friendly terms with Fathers Frois and Organtino. That he should have met personally with the fathers on the occasion of Cabral's visit, and even seated himself at the same table, was considered quite extraordinary. Stories were also told of Father Frois's first trip to Gifu, when the Signore had had his own sons, still boys at the time, serve refreshments to the priest. Even taking into account a natural inclination to be hospitable to guests from a distant land, something here was utterly different from his behavior toward his own vassals and retainers.

The impression that I for one had of the Signore was of a man who was sensitive, intellectual, and introspective, without a trace of brutality, coarseness, or vulgarity. He was fond of jests, and despite my painfully slow Japanese would listen patiently as I recounted one or the other of the romances I had learned in Genoa. When I reached the end of a story—particularly one wherein, for example, a priest who had been disporting himself with a woman was finally thrashed and driven off—the Signore would laugh quite merrily. Occasionally, he would himself tell a similar sort of story—I could never imagine where he had learned them—and at such times a natural good humor would invade his face, along with a certain self-satisfaction at the effect his story was having on his audience. The Japanese present on such occasions saw it as an utter mystery that this side of the Signore's character, which he had never shown to any of them, should be brought out by foreigners such as ourselves. One explanation they offered stemmed in part from an incident that occurred during the attack on Ishiyama (another battle which I shall describe for you presently). At that time, Father Joan Francisco, who had just arrived in Japan, was detained by the Signore at his camp, where they were said to have engaged in the most earnest exchanges. The rumor went out that the Signore had become a Christian, and some quite respectable sources were said to have given it credence.

If I were to hazard my own explanation for the undeniable change that overcame the Signore in the presence of those who were not his compatriots, I would say it had to do, first of all, with the very fact that we *were* strangers, and thus so little tied to the Signore's world. Clearly there was no need to overawe us, nor in our presence did he feel the need to personify discipline and strength—as he apparently did in the company of his countrymen and subjects. One might, I suppose, argue exactly the opposite: that as ruler and representative of the Japanese kingdom, he should have felt compelled to ensure that we regarded him with sufficient respect (such indeed had been the attitude of rulers I knew of in Nuova Spagna and the Molucca Islands), but such considerations never seemed to bother him. It is true that his extraordinary interest in weapons, tactics, navigation, and all manner of other arts and sciences did in part explain his affability toward us. Yet it seemed to me that the ultimate reason for his friendliness lay elsewhere, in the fact that we harbored no preconceptions about his person, so that he might deal with us, and we with him, simply as human beings. I have noted, for example, that the great majority of his retainers turned pale at the very mention of his name; if he chanced to pass in their general vicinity, they would throw themselves on the ground and not so much as look up until he had gone. Summoned into his presence or otherwise directly addressed, they would most likely remain silent as mutes, foreheads pressed against the floor. Even the twenty or thirty retainers who were constantly in attendance on the Signore seldom ventured anything approaching spontaneous conversation. At best, they made the most conventional replies to the Signore's remarks, in a strangely stilted manner devoid of all life and wit.

I knew that the Signore generally slept alone in a room with wooden floors, rather than one with straw matting. I wondered whether there were not perhaps a few days each month that he spent with his wife and children, but it seemed more probable that he was too preoccupied with responsibilities, ambitions, and crises to let himself relax even briefly. In the final analysis, he was living proof of the adage that the soul that seeks to rise above the common herd is perforce a lonely one.

In the Signore's case, however, I do not feel that the cause of his loneliness lay only with himself. I had seen how those around him were quite unable to recognize his human qualities—either his strengths or his weaknesses—and imposed on him instead fearsome images of their own creation. I could not help feeling that the gloomy, chilly atmosphere that surrounded him was less a product of his own character than something others had, however unintentionally, fabricated around him.

And over and against this grim atmosphere, there was his mood when around us, his visitors from afar. Though he might be the cruelest of kings, with us he was also just one man among many, with all the frailties that that implied. The greatest of men are not without their softer side. Brave Cortés was bewitched by the beauty of jewels, and the cool, calculating Cosimo de' Medici could be reduced to tears by a lovely miniature. The Signore, too, had his human side; it may be that our very recognition of this fact accounted for the difference—for the indulgence—in his dealings with us. Why, otherwise, should he have gone out of his way to call me to court on more than one occasion? Why, later, when the seminary at Azuchi had been constructed, should he have come so often, at all hours of the day and night, to talk with Organtino or me? Doubtless he was accustomed to isolation at court and formality in his dealings with his subjects. Possibly, even, he preferred, in the long run, the mathematical clarity of military strategies or government policy to dealings with men. Yet it also seems conceivable that, perhaps without realizing it himself, he longed for a kind of sociability, one founded on sensitivity and correct behavior. Even now, at a distance of ten years and a thousand leagues, I am almost certain that such was indeed the case.

It was Lord Hashiba, perhaps, who most readily perceived this inner desire of the Signore's. He was a small, dark-skinned man with large eyes, in no sense distinguished in appearance yet filled with a mysterious vitality. He had considerable intelligence and was cheerful and frank by nature, if a trifle cantankerous. Even assuming he could indeed see into the Signore's heart, he never said as much, but pretended to know nothing and confined his conversation with the Signore to the most trivial of everyday matters:

"The Signore has gained some weight recently," or "The Signore appears to have lost some weight." "He is perhaps eating too much," or "Perhaps you eat too little."

On occasion, the Signore would criticize Hashiba for the lack of matter in his speech, but it seemed to me that these rebukes were just part of a game between the two; the more severe the reprimands, the deeper the Signore's affection for Hashiba seemed to grow. It might also be added that as a practitioner of the art of military strategy, Hashiba was the superior of any of the other principal vassals, a talent that no doubt helped endear him with the Signore. It may surprise you to hear, my friend, that this remarkable man was not the scion of some great family, but of the humblest origins—his parents being, I believe, mere peasants. The heights to which he had risen despite this will give some idea of his intelligence and ability.

Within a year or so of my arrival in Gifu, I had, naturally enough, gained a certain understanding of the system of vassalage in this kingdom. I had not, of course, been introduced personally to all of the important vassals owing fealty to the Signore, but I had gathered a good deal about their positions by their deportment at court, the seats they were allotted, and the Signore's attitude toward them. My various mentors had also given their own accounts of the relative positions and relationships of the grandees. Combining my own observations and hints such as these, I had concluded that the important vassals, generals, and *daimyos* could be divided into three distinct factions: first, the vassals who had been with the Signore since the time when he was governor of Owari (for example, Hashiba); second, the *daimyos* and vassals who had come under the Signore's authority as he expanded his dominion; and third, the *daimyos*, hidalgoes, and *samurai* who maintained close ties with the Kubo-sama—the *governatore* of Kyoto—and interested themselves principally in classical studies and literature. The latter were also, generally, the most sympathetic to the Christian church.

There were, of course, men who seemed to have no part in any of these factions, and others who might have been said to belong to more than one. Sakuma, for example, would have had to be included in the first group, but was also a candidate for the third insofar as he was quite sympathetic to the Christians. In general, however, it was convenient to think in terms of three factions whose members shared certain common interests. When I first formulated this scheme, I explained it to Organtino and he said that his view was much the same.

Of the three factions, it was, naturally enough, the first that had the most intimate ties to the Signore, but where military strategy and the administration of the realm were concerned he tended to place his confidence in the men of the third faction. Though I never fully understood the nature of this relationship, or why these men should have been willing to put their talents to use in the service of a master who was not their own, it seemed to me that, having been born in an age when the court of the emperor in Kyoto—the figurehead ruler to whom they owed their principal allegiance—was in decline, they had no recourse but to serve the man who wielded real power if they wished to demonstrate their abilities as strategists and statesmen. Moreover, bowed as they were under the heavy weight of a family tradition that had become nearly meaningless, they were already accustomed to selling themselves and their talents to the Kubo-sama. They were, one might say, nobles reduced to a state of genteel poverty, and, like their brothers in the courts of Europe, they made their way in the world well enough by observing the proper courtesies and exercising a good measure of calculated self-interest. The interest in Christianity that these men shared, and their personal friendship with Frois and Organtino, were due to the fact that their position as "men of culture" required that they show an interest in new religions and ideas.

On this score, the relationship was decidedly different from the friendship between the Signore and the priests. The Signore cared little about the priests' official role. He had of course heard the teachings of the church concerning, for example, the creation and the immortality of the soul, but he took them merely as one among many possible explanations; as he had declared to Frois at their first meeting, he could believe in nothing that could not be seen with the eyes, and valued only that which could be shown to accord with the principles of reason. The Signore's continuing good will toward Frois and Organtino had nothing to do with their beliefs; rather, it seemed, he respected the zeal and sincerity that had led them to risk body and soul, to brave "a thousand leagues of salt spray," in order to come to a distant land and bear witness to those beliefs. He had said as much on more than one occasion. Familiar as he was with isolation, he doubtless understood better than any of his subjects the loneliness and suffering that faced them in a foreign land.

When, as was often the case, he took the Buddhist clergy to task, he always compared them with the Jesuit fathers. Unlike the Japanese priests, he said, the foreigners never came begging for anything. Though I was not, I fear, always in complete agreement with the Signore's opinion of the church, I too had been conscious of the kind of lives these particular representatives of that body led, and of the flame of sympathy they had lit in the Signore's breast. For the most part, they had my admiration as well. They could hardly have been unaware that—as was apparent even to one as little concerned with the church as I— many of their brothers in faith were walking more comfortable paths, some leading to power and influence in Rome, some to a life of drinking wine and growing fat in some rural parish such as Abruzzi. Yet they themselves had chosen a very different path.

Thus while the Signore was drawn to the severity and discipline of the Christian life, these men of the third faction were more attracted by Christian love and charity. Though well enough disposed toward the church in general, the Signore did not exhibit the least interest in doctrines of divine mercy or providence. Nor, in his own affairs, as I am sure I have made amply plain, did he show any trace of mercy for his enemies. This fact, indeed, gave rise to more than a little discontent, not only among the Christian *daimyo*s and *samurai*s and sympathizers, but also among some of the chief vassals who found it difficult to fathom why it was necessary to slay an opponent who was begging for mercy and making all suitable signs of submission. A battle, they felt, should end with the enemy's surrender, not with his slaughter. Among their number, Lords Sakuma, Takayama, Araki, Akechi, and Hosokawa in particular would have favored more leniency than was provided for under the Signore's unbending law. One day, I heard, this difference of outlook inspired him to lecture Sakuma to the following effect:

"Once you have joined battle with an enemy, you must aspire to victory and nothing else. The fighting in itself can never be the goal, only the victory. You may feel that it is only human to show mercy to an enemy once you have him at a disadvantage. But battle, by its very nature, is an arena in which no mercy may rightfully be expected. The purpose of war is victory over the opponent, and final victory comes only when one puts the opponent to the sword. Where mercy is shown, it may be that there was no reason for the battle in the first place. Indeed, if you believe that mercy is the proper part of man, why, pray, should you make war at all? And as for the precious opponent whom you would spare, what would you call a man who sues for peace when he sees he cannot possibly hope for victory? I, for one, would call him a coward and a rogue. What business has a man who has just been seeking your destruction with all his might to begin chattering about compassion? Once it comes to war, you must persist in the ways of war to the end, regardless of how your own fortunes may fall.

"It is no different for a carpenter building a house: from first to last, the house is the point. Or for the painter who takes up his brush: the picture is all, from the first stroke to the last. The man who plots a strategy for a battle is like the carpenter who cuts wood and fits joints. The soldier wielding his lance is no different from the painter wielding his brush. Any carelessness or laziness in the soldier, and inevitably the army will suffer the humiliation of defeat. Likewise, the lazy carpenter or painter will suffer his own sort of disgrace.

"In any endeavor, whether or not things develop as they should and come to their fullness depends on seeking the way of reason with one's whole heart. A person truly worthy of the name of master—of carpentry, painting, or whatever else—must pursue his art unrelentingly. He must seek after reason and rely upon himself. Only through such single-minded effort does anything of value come into existence. Once this has happened, others take it up, the thing of value is recognized as such, and the original master is acknowledged. But it is the singleness of mind and the devotion to reason that matter.

"A soldier in battle is much the same. He eschews all thoughts of mercy, just as a painter thinks only of his painting. The painter who turns aside from the way of the brush cannot hope to summon the spirits of the great painters. How then can the soldier who puts aside the way of the sword hope to be able to call upon the spirit of the warrior? To be able to summon this spirit, you must forego the idea of compassion as being wholly incompatible with your one avowed purpose. He who meets his enemy in battle must, if he is worthy of the name of warrior, annihilate him without mercy. Such a man and only such a man will take his place of honor as a true soldier."

Whether it was indeed to Lord Sakuma that this speech was

made, or whether it was to some other one of his vassals, I cannot say with certainty. But I am sure that he used either these words or others like them, for I myself heard him say much the same thing on other occasions. As for his choice of metaphors, the Signore's great respect for master craftsmen and artists was well known. He extended them generous protection so that they could concentrate on their work even in time of war, and from time to time was known to give them lavish rewards for particular achievements.

Having set down the above lengthy speech by the Signore, it occurs to me that there is no more apt phrase to sum up his philosophy and the nature of his actions than the one he uses here—*koto ga naru*—namely, the notion that "things must develop as they should and come to their proper fullness." He believed that if a thing did not proceed in a completely rational manner, then it could not possibly achieve the completeness for which it was intended. It is necessary, I feel, to understand that he willfully overrode his own sensitivity (and if I had been called upon to defend him against those of his countrymen who cursed him as a cruel demon, I might simply have said that I have never known a man of such fine sensibilities) in line with the principle of necessary and rational fruition—that is, for the purpose of becoming the true master warrior. In making himself impervious to human feelings, he chose a path fraught with every difficulty life could bring; and the further he walked along that path, the less he was understood by those around him.

Precisely because he applied his precepts to himself with such severity, he felt justified in holding others to them as well, and in meting out the severest penalties—even death—for anyone, of whatever class or station, who betrayed the slightest sign of carelessness or laziness in discharging his appointed task. Perhaps the most striking example of this fearful consistency was related to me by Father Frois. It seems that a group of ladies-in-waiting, delegated to watch over the Signore's quarters in his absence, went instead to visit some shrine or temple. When their laxness was discovered by the Signore, they paid for the lapse with their heads.

I hope it will not seem that my apologia for the Signore's actions is due to the good will he showed me personally. It is true that after the seminary at Azuchi was completed he would drop in on occasion to hear the music, or to laugh at Organtino's cheerful jests, or to have me tell long seafaring tales. In the same way, he would attempt to master the use of the telescope, or question me about the means of attacking a fortress with mortars and all manner of other similar things. Yet what remains most strongly in my mind is not such personal courtesies, but the conviction that among all the Japanese people I met during my stay in that land, I never knew one who believed as strongly as he that the greatest good was that all things should come about necessarily and reasonably. Whether in galloping across the countryside with only a small band in attendance, or dressing himself simply with a minimum of ornament, his every action was informed by his belief in this principle.

It occurs to me now that the attraction this philosophy held for me lay in its resemblance to a truth one learns from the sea, where danger, loneliness, and hunger teach that the only things of importance are the most basic ones, and that there is wisdom simply in stripping things of all that is extraneous. Please do not think it fond exaggeration, dear friend, when I say that at times I saw in this Signore my other self. To me, he was not simply a great general or a superior politician, but a man who possessed a will to seek the limits of perfection in the work he had chosen for himself. And it was in precisely this kind of will—like a meteor hurtling bright through the void, straining to pierce the sky—that I myself found the only meaning of our life here on this earth.

It was said in that country that from the time of his youth, on

82

the rare occasions when he was flushed with a little wine, he liked
to dance, holding a fan, and to sing this song:

> To think that a man
> has but fifty years under heaven;
> surely this world
> seems but a vain dream.

He had faced up to the futility of the world, nor could it be said
that he set much stock in dreams. He was a man intent on confronting the void, challenging death, and probing the limits of his
own will.

It was at the end of fifteen seventy-four that I received a letter
from Organtino, who was then in Kyoto. Around that time, the
Signore and his advisers were conferring in Gifu on the best way
to deal with the armies to the east now that the rebels at
Nagashima had been destroyed. The drilling of the musket companies had been intensified, and following the practical demonstration given by my arquebus corps of the progress it had
made, the new strategy of triple file firing with advances and
retreats had been adopted by all the musket companies. If Organtino had not called me back to Kyoto just then, I would no doubt
have been able to participate in the battle with the Takeda army
in the east, and would perhaps have been able to describe for you
firsthand the spectacular exploits of the musket companies in the
battle of Nagashino—exploits that were later to be bruited the
length of the land from Kyoto down to distant Satsuma.
However, when I thought of all the new difficulties Organtino
must be facing in Kyoto since our parting, I knew that I could no
longer continue in my role as military adviser at Gifu.

Frois and Organtino had been hard at work day and night in
the capital, as I knew both from Organtino's letters and from the
messengers who came to Gifu from time to time. In one sense, I
had a better idea of the activities of the mission as a whole than I

had while in Kyoto, thanks largely to the detailed information I received when *daimyos* sympathetic to Christianity came calling at court. (Lords Sakuma, Takayama, Araki, Shibata, and Murai in particular were quite helpful here.) These reports, unfortunately, suggested that Organtino was still working beyond the limits of his bodily strength. Sometimes, I realized, the absence of his name from the official reports meant that he was ill again. Occasionally, a message would state quite plainly that he was sick.

After the exile of Kubo-sama, it seemed, the city had enjoyed a peaceful spell, and the fathers had succeeded in converting several *daimyos* of the Gokinai provinces to Christianity. This meant that someone, either Frois or Organtino, had to be making a constant round of their castles. Nor was the task any easier for the one who stayed behind in the city, since work there continued unabated. There was Mass to be held in the early morning, then other devotions before noon. Next came litanies for funerals and sundry other rites, followed by sermons to be preached to the faithful. After afternoon devotions, there was more preaching on various offices of the church, and special sermons for the heathen. Next, the confessions of those preparing to become Christians were heard; the number of such people was increasing daily, and at times the priests could not even find time for meals. After all this, Father Frois spent much of his night writing long reports to Goa or working on one of his scholarly projects. He admitted that there were nights when he was so absorbed in his writing that he was unaware of the light of dawn creeping into his room. Although Organtino did not have the strength for this kind of labor, he devoted all the energy he had to the study of the Japanese language, while continuing to visit the sick and the destitute. Not uncommonly, he was summoned to the home of a heathen, whither he would go as readily as anywhere else.

It was Organtino's custom, on such forays out into the city, to wear black robes like those of a Buddhist monk, with straw sandals on his bare feet. To us his appearance was, to say the least, somewhat peculiar. It also seemed to strike the Japanese as quite strange, and some of the congregation said they would prefer that he dress in a way more befitting a padre—that is, in a black Portuguese cape with a broad-brimmed hat. Organtino himself, however, dismissed their suggestions with a laugh, saying simply that his "Barbarian Priest" costume was in practice the best means of overcoming the fears and wariness of the people of Japan. One day, however, when I pressed him, he offered the following explanation:

"First of all, the Japanese may easily see from this costume that I am a priest, and that I and my brothers live a priestly life. The familiar robes, in short, tell them that we are men of God. And with luck, the sense of familiarity inspired by the robes may blossom into something akin to good will. These people, in every respect so gentle and retiring, seem to derive a certain satisfaction from the sight of a foreigner going out of his way to follow their customs and wear their *quimonos*. At the same time my appearance, as you can well see, is something of a jest—in fact positively eccentric. Being sensitive to that sort of thing, these good people will readily laugh at me, and the laughter becomes a kind of sympathy, or even affection, for the foreigner who makes a joke of himself in a silly attempt to become acquainted with their ways."

It seemed to me that this shrewd practicality owed much to Organtino's peasant heritage, and I was more than a little impressed with his reasoning. Though he differed here from Father Frois, there was no lack of evidence for the effectiveness of his approach. This humble, unceremonious man had earned the friendship of citizens in every part of the city. Even those who did not go so far as to become Christians themselves seemed to return Organtino's infinite good will in kind. Gathering around him as he oversaw the distribution of rice gruel on the banks of the river, they would question him endlessly:

"Where were you born?" "Is it farther away than Tenjiku [by which they meant India]?" "What do the people there eat?" "Are there mountains in your country?" "What sort of cities do you have there?" "Do the people trade with one another?" "Do they fight wars?" And so on.

A long time since, and even without Father Cabral's criticisms, the extreme inconvenience of continuing to conduct services and give instruction in the dilapidated, drafty old church had become apparent to the priests. Thus a decision had been made to reconstruct the church—as many of the Japanese parishioners had been hoping for some time—thereby demonstrating by external show as well as by good works the magnificence and benevolence of our Lord's church. There had first been an attempt to purchase a Buddhist temple for use as a church, but it had ended in failure. Finally, a decision was reached by clergy and congregation together to construct a completely new church. The letter continued:

"I may never have told you, my friend, that before entering the theological school in Brescia, I was apprenticed to a carpenter. And though I would not pretend to emulate Saint Thomas, at university I studied the science of architecture. Thus my enthusiasm for the project of building a church was partly due from the outset to a certain confidence in our chances of success. Nor has that confidence been diminished to any great degree. Nevertheless, I am beginning to be concerned about what might happen were I unable to see the project through to completion. I fear, frankly, that I may lack the strength to draw up plans and oversee the construction while continuing with my clerical responsibilities. I believe you know, good friend, that I am not one to fear either hard work or illness. What troubles me is that, should I be unable to supervise its construction, the church might not be realized in the way we have envisioned it. My heart, you see, is set on building a church that resembles our churches in Europe down to the last detail. There are various obstacles at present to our plans—difficulties with funds and supplies, the lack of proper carpenters and other workers—but I am confident we could find ways of overcoming them. My one concern is that the whole of our efforts will come to naught if I am incapacitated and there is no one else here with a knowledge of the art of building as practiced in our homeland.

"It has occurred to me, however, that you, my friend, are quite well versed in this field—are, in fact, most familiar with the construction of churches in Europe. Thus I have been thinking, ever since we began work on the plans, of asking if you might return to Kyoto as soon as possible, to ensure that the new church is completed according to plan—and to relieve me, I confess, of my anxiety. Father Frois will be sending a formal request to the Signore to that effect, so if you are willing, please come to help with the building. It would be most gratifying if you could arrange to come as soon as possible. . . ."

As I finished reading Organtino's letter, I was aware that I should have returned to Kyoto long ago. The problem remained of whether the Signore would permit my departure in view of the imminent threat from the Takeda army in the east. My arquebus corps, however, had at Nagashima already more than proved its effectiveness, while the members of the corps had subsequently been assigned to various companies in order to train others in the techniques of loading and firing. In short, it seemed that my usefulness to the Signore was, for the moment, at an end. The fact that he complied with the request and sent me to Kyoto was due no doubt to such considerations. He gave a farewell banquet for me with several of his chief vassals in attendance, and took the occasion to present me with a sword decorated with intricate carvings.

The day after the banquet, I left Gifu with an escort of twelve mounted soldiers, and the following morning we rode past the lake of Omi. It surface was smooth, like a mirror reflecting the cold winter sky.

On arriving in Kyoto, I hurried straight to the church. Organtino embraced me, his eyes bright with tears.

"What a blessing that I did not send you away when we were at Shiki," he murmured.

The old church was unchanged, though perhaps even livelier than ever. Members of the congregation were rehearsing hymns. Women were cleaning the sanctuary, and there was an old woman praying. The children were trailing about after the friars. Organtino had got together several of the chief carpenters come to work on the new church. As he explained the drawings, they would nod, then whisper together for a while or stand with arms folded, lost in thought. I conferred briefly with them myself, then immediately set to studying the details of the plans: the dimensions, the arrangement of rooms, the structural specifications, the roof trussing, the windows, the exterior decorations, and so forth. The carpenters proved both extremely diligent and modest in manner, quick to comprehend what was wanted of them and with an almost uncanny ability to adapt to unfamiliar tasks. Nevertheless, in spite of such able workmen and the enthusiasm with which Organtino had drawn up the plans, it still took us a full year to complete preparations for the building. There were many additional drawings required, which I myself made in consultation with Organtino, and when these were finished, we had to go around visiting the lords of the Gokinai provinces to explain our plan and canvass for wood and stone. Transporting the materials entailed considerable difficulty, and we often met with the local authorities and members of the church to work out details concerning porters, provisions, and lodging for the workers.

It was in May of the following year, fifteen hundred and seventy-five, that a startling message came from Gifu: the army of the Takeda lord had been destroyed in a battle at Nagashino. One passage in the account in particular, beginning "The valiant activities of the gun companies...," impressed me deeply. How I would have loved to see that glorious victory with my own eyes! But the outcome of the battle itself seemed only natural; had I had the benefit of just one of the Signore's disciplined corps of marksmen in the jungles of Nuova Spagna, all my difficulties there might have been solved.

Yet my only real regret at being in Kyoto was that I no longer had occasion to talk to the Signore. Had I been there at the battle of Nagashino, we would almost certainly have reviewed the engagement in minute detail, and on that basis might have collaborated on some new strategy. I must admit that, had it not been for Organtino, I would have felt little inclination to spend my time in the procurement of building materials or in making arrangements for their transportation. If my expertise and energies, such as they were, helped at all in the building of the church, it was for the sake of that plump, good-natured, childlike peasant from Brescia. To see him bustling about the chores of construction, his round nose dripping with perspiration, was to feel somehow that my regrets at not taking part in the battle were quite insignificant.

We began assembling our materials at the end of the year, and construction was started early in the spring of fifteen hundred and seventy-six. Our principal patrons were the vassals of the third faction who, as I have told you, were either themselves Christians or were very much in sympathy with the church. One of the most generous was Lord Takayama. Upon seeing the plans, he personally went to encourage the carpenters. He also took it upon himself to supply much of the lumber, and visited the forests of his domain to urge the woodcutters to do their best. Horses were used to drag the timber from the mountains to the river, where it was loaded onto boats for the journey to Kyoto. Takayama personally supervised the work at each stage, sending his son, Ukon, instead whenever he could not be present himself.

Our chief difficulty during the construction proved to be assembling a sufficient number of workers. At this time, the Signore had already begun work on a grand palace at Azuchi, and very few artisans of any great skill were available for other enterprises. We lacked, in particular, carpenters, plasterers, and stonemasons. Nevertheless, whenever we found ourselves in particular difficulty, Takayama would send us all the available workers from his own province, and also exercise his powers of persuasion on other *daimyos* who had shown themselves not unfriendly to our cause. In this manner, we always seemed to have just enough hands to do the work.

The enthusiasm of the Japanese Christians who had come to help with the building was quite extraordinary. The organization of the faithful was put to full use in mobilizing help not only from the congregation in Kyoto but also from neighboring provinces. They worked in a methodical fashion, apportioning tasks, drawing up schedules, and fixing working hours. Men were sent out to procure rice and provisions, while others went to purchase lumber and recruit craftsmen.

We were the recipients, too, of various material donations. Some Christian women would send bundles containing golden combs or gorgeous *quimonos* as donations. A certain *samurai* who happened to visit our building site removed the gold handguard from his blade and added it to the collection. The wealthy warriors and merchants not only donated valuables and large sums of money, but also arranged among themselves to provide refreshments for the workers, each taking his turn.

The poorer citizens gave what they could. A man sent some rope he had braided himself, and another came barefoot from distant Tamba bringing a handful of nails. One man brought a few planks, and a woman donated cotton cloth she had woven at home to be used for the carpenters' clothing. An old woman offered a few handfuls of rice to help feed the workers. A peasant brought the iron kettle from her kitchen, and an elderly *samurai* gave us armor and silk robes that had belonged to his dead son as an offering for the repose of his soul. The widow of a merchant gave some coppers she had been hoarding away for years. There were many others besides, nor were they all Christians. Among the donors were many heathens who had chanced, for example, to meet the amiable Organtino by the river or in the streets of the capital. They came to bring a few pieces of silver or to take a turn working on the church. The father, it seems, had touched their sympathies in some manner.

Naturally enough, perhaps, there were other, less friendly reactions to the building of a church, and in fact disturbances at the site were not uncommon. Harassment of the workers included frequent stone-throwing and shouted insults, but the injuries thus incurred were never serious, so we did not make an issue of them. Occasionally, lumber and stones were stolen during the night, or tools would disappear, so the members of the church assigned watches to stand guard, and the new governor of Kyoto, Lord Murai, was sufficiently concerned to send some soldiers as well.

Murai was a gentle, portly man who was ever mindful of the Signore's wishes, and spared no effort in seeing our needs were met. Not only did he exempt us from the taxes normally levied on materials brought into Kyoto, but he diligently sought solutions to all our problems, from the kind I have already mentioned down to the petty inconveniences arising during the construction. He often visited the site himself, and when his observant eyes discovered an aspect of our work that differed from traditional Japanese methods, he would question Organtino or myself about it at length. It was in large part due to help given by this courteous old gentleman that the work proceeded ahead of schedule.

As I have said, the generosity of the great lords in the vicinity of Kyoto was reflected in every aspect of the work, but there was one particular kindness, involving Lord Murai, that caused us considerable amusement whenever we recalled it in later times. We had carried out, with proper ceremony, the raising of the ridgepole (which I will describe for you presently), when it suddenly became clear to those who came to view the building just what sort of structure it was to be—that is, a full three stories high and towering over the buildings around it. One day soon thereafter, the elders of Kyoto got together and came to seek an audience with Murai demanding cancellation of the permit to build the church. The structure, exceeding the prescribed limit of two stories, would look down on houses and temples alike, a prospect they found offensive, even scandalous. And they asked that the building be demolished straightway. The good-natured Murai's response was said to have been follows:

"Gentlemen, I understand your concern, but I think you are being most unfair. Consider, now: the very fact that these foreigners have chosen our city in which to build their church means that Kyoto is gaining yet another notable sight, and to have a building in the foreign style—why, that is more wonderful still. Rather than castigating them, should we not see their activities as a boon, and honor them accordingly? But to deal more directly with your objection, have you not considered their reasons for building to such a height? Might those reasons not have to do with the cramped conditions in that quarter? They are simply looking to take fullest advantage of the site, and it is incumbent on you, as their neighbors, to recognize this. Finally, good Sirs, if you really feel so strongly that taller buildings are undesirable in our city, I would suggest you pull down all buildings currently standing which exceed the limit. When you have agreed to that condition, then I will consider dismantling the Christian church."

The elders concluded forthwith that they had no hope of persuading the governor, so they came to us directly, on the authority of the city council, to order demolition of the "excessively tall" portion of the church. Our rebuttal was as follows:

"If a building of such height was contrary to your wishes, why were we not told so before the start of construction? We can only suppose that your failure to object in advance was due to the fact that we had already presented our plans to the Signore in Gifu and to the governor here in Kyoto, and had received their approval. Furthermore, you ask us to reduce the height of the building by one story, but our structure is not in the style of your temples and pagodas. That is to say, the upper story is not merely a cottage set on the roof of the building beneath it. The whole is integrally related in such a way that removing the upper portions would require altering the entire building and result in considerable expense. Thus, since the requisite building permit was issued in accordance with due procedure, we feel confident in saying that we have no responsibility to comply with your request. We should warn you, in addition, that if any measures are taken on your part to destroy the building, we will immediately ask the Signore at Gifu and the governor of this city to deal with you as they see fit."

In the face of this strong show of resolve, upward of forty of the most worthy of the burghers assembled a veritable mountain of gifts, planning to go directly to the court at Azuchi to press their petition. (Though Organtino had spoken of the "Signore at Gifu," it was, in fact, in the spring of that very year that the court had moved to the new palace at Azuchi.) It was widely rumored that the good citizens of Kyoto had been incited to such extremes by the Buddhist priests of the capital, and that the latter were not

93

merely intent on having the building permit revoked but were spreading slander against the Christians and scheming to have the padres and their congregation driven from the city.

I do not now recall clearly who alerted us to such rumors, but once we were aware of them it seemed imperative that someone should reach Azuchi before the elders. Lorenzo himself, he said, was not up to such a hurried journey on horseback, so a young Japanese friar named Paolo was sent without delay, bearing letters to the Signore from Frois and Organtino. His departure preceded that of the elders of Kyoto by two full days. At Azuchi, he met with several of the *daimyos* of the third faction who chanced to be at court and explained our dilemma to them, but they merely laughed and told him to urge the padres not to worry, as matters were well in hand.

"Even if by any unlikely chance this slander should reach the Signore's ears," they told him with supreme confidence, "we intend to make sure that you will suffer no trouble thereby."

But it was of Lord Murai's kindness in particular that I had intended to tell you. He had, it seems, received his own reports that the elders were on their way to Azuchi, and, braving the chill of early spring despite his age, hurried to Azuchi himself, first on horseback and then by special boat. Aware of the Signore's partiality to foreigners, he did not want the fact of Kyoto's antipathy to them made known to his lord in too blatant a fashion.

You may well imagine the surprise of the elders themselves when, arriving at Azuchi and entering the court, they saw the smiling face of their kindly governor. It seems they still persisted in trying to have their petition brought before the Signore, but in the end were unable to find a single courtier willing to speak on their behalf.

"The very sight of the expressions on their faces was indeed a blessing," said Paolo. "It is said that they did not even dare return to Kyoto by daylight, but were forced to slip in like thieves after dark."

But I am anticipating myself again. As I said earlier, these events took place following the raising of the ridgepole, an event which we celebrated as spring was coming to an end.

This great beam that was to be the center of the whole structure and support its entire weight had been made from a colossal tree cut in one of Lord Takayama's forests. It was extremely long and heavy, and we had calculated that seven hundred men would be needed to lift it into place, a task that was to be accomplished with a good deal of ceremony.

We were making final preparations at the site when a message came from the governor to the effect that, should there be a shortage of able bodies, he would immediately dispatch as many as a thousand men; and a high-ranking *samurai*, a distant relative of his, was sent to attend the pole-raising ceremony. This representative and the numerous attendants who accompanied him bearing saké, fruit, sweets, and sundry other comestibles all wore splendid robes. Meanwhile, people were examining the pole, checking the fit of its joints, and testing the strength of the ropes that would be used to lift it.

As the moment when the pole was to be raised drew nearer, men began stripping to the waist. Some spit in their palms and rubbed them with dirt, others stretched and stomped to warm themselves, still others began tugging at the ropes. People were laughing, shouting, and jostling one another in their excitement; some were even weeping. There were men seated on the ground patiently waiting, perhaps passing the time by guessing the weight of the beam, and others scrambling to find a place on the rope. Everyone was waiting for the voice of the chief carpenter.

In addition to the workers, several thousand citizens from the surrounding districts had come to witness the event, adding to the noise and confusion. The majority of them were heathens favorably disposed, it seemed, to the building of a church. Some from the immediate neighborhood came bearing congratulatory gifts, their previous antipathies apparently forgotten. They seemed inordinately pleased that their district had gained the admiration of all Kyoto.

Finally, the raising of the pole began and a cheer went up from the crowd. At a signal from the chief carpenter, all arms strained in unison. The great, thick ropes pulled taut like the warp of an enormous loom, and as they did so a shout arose from the men. The chief carpenter shouted in response, thus setting up a rhythm repeated again and again as they pulled on the ropes. The beam seemed to come to life, to stir itself slowly from the ground. Gently it swayed upward, the carpenter's chant alternating with the shouts of the men. The chief carpenter's voice, the clipped cry of the men, the carpenter's voice, the cry again—only louder now, as the spectators joined in encouragingly.

"*Yoo-i-jo! Do-quei-jo!*" they cried again and again, and each time the beam inched slowly, almost painfully, up into the air. Now and again it would sway slightly as if it had momentarily become quite light, then would jerk up a little more and the ropes on the other side would gradually be pulled taut. When the whole process had been repeated several times more, the beam was at last in place, and was fixed on the cylindrical columns that were to support it. It was then connected to a second beam which had been raised by another team. Suddenly, the structure seemed to acquire a certain solidity.

In quick succession the third and fourth beams were raised into place and secured to the center beam. The carpenters worked high up in the air, like birds perched on slender branches. Finally, at a signal from the chief carpenter, several hundred ropes were detached at once and fell to earth, and the beams and pillars that would soon be part of a church stood like a huge stick horse. It was no more than the skeleton of a building, yet there was the feeling that something that had not existed heretofore had suddenly come into being. The crowd stood silent for a moment, transfixed, then from among the workers a great, triumphant cheer went up and spread to the onlookers. Frois and Organtino, the friars, and the rest of the believers knelt and offered a lengthy prayer of thanksgiving.

With the raising of the ridgepole, the building was, in its essentials, laid out before us. From now on, work at the site became more lively and purposeful than ever. From early morning, the sounds of nails being hammered and boards being planed could be heard both inside and outside. The exterior walls were painted, and Portuguese plaster was used to form the decorations on the eaves and cornices. As the plans will bear witness, it was our intention—Organtino's and mine—that the church should be more Italian than Portuguese where its form, the style of the portico, the façade, eaves, windows, and all the other exterior embellishments were concerned. Due to the limitations of the site, it was not possible to erect a proper basilica, so that the final building was square in shape and somewhat gloomy in aspect. Yet in its fundamentals, I feel safe in saying, our church was the equal of some in Rome.

The first Mass was held in the church on the fifteenth day of August, fifteen hundred and seventy-six. The plaster decorations on the ceiling were not yet complete, but Organtino felt work had progressed to a point where the church could be dedicated; he gave it the name "Church of the Ascension." The sound of hymns echoed among the still-exposed roof beams, and there was barely an eye in the congregation that was not brimming with tears. The church overflowed with people come to hear Organtino's sermon—by this time delivered in the finest Japanese—and the gilt cross atop the bell tower shone in the sun. This cross could be seen far and wide in the city, and was said to be a source of great pride to believers in the outlying villages.

During the building of the church I had made the acquaintance of several of the *daimyo*s of the region: Takayama and his son Ukon, Araki, and Sakuma; all of them gentle, dignified men. Lord Takayama was small and rather thin, and getting along in years. He bore numerous scars on his face, neck, and arms which he viewed as reminders of a youth squandered foolishly on the field of battle—a particular embarrassment, he used to say, when he recalled that they had once been a source of great pride.

It was natural perhaps that, as a devout Christian, Takayama should be sympathetic to our cause; but so were Araki and Sakuma—heathens both—who were as solicitous of Frois and Organtino as Wada had been before them. Of the two, Sakuma was the taller, a placid and soft-spoken man more like a scholar than a commander on the field of battle. Had he been born in Genoa, he might have been the president of the city council.

By contrast, Araki was a short old man with a swarthy complexion and broad shoulders. He was well known for being quick-tempered in both word and deed, and quite stubborn. When he was excited, his head had an odd way of wobbling on his neck. For the most part, though, he was a moderate and rather cheerful man. Once or twice I went with Organtino to visit his castle, and the life he led there seemed in many ways to be the essence of happiness. His elderly wife was an elegant woman of perfectly erect bearing, and the two old people were surrounded by beautiful daughters and numerous grandchildren. Lord Araki was often to be seen holding one of the younger children, rubbing cheeks with it or sticking out his tongue to amuse it.

During my stay in Japan, I saw similar caresses and expressions of fondness fairly regularly among the humbler classes, but I am sure I never saw the like among the warrior class, particularly among its more exalted members. As a rule, a child of this class was taught what was right and what was wrong by a kind of catechizing just as soon as it gained the power of speech. Children ten years of age were addressed as though they were quite grown up; often we were obliged to marvel at the reasonableness of these children, the likes of whom are not to be found in any of the kingdoms of Europe. Indeed, such children were among our greatest sources of wonder in all the kingdom of Japan.

Within the mansion of Araki, though, children regained their natural vivacity, audacity, and cheerfulness, and their boisterousness incurred not a single word of rebuke from any quarter. Even as we spoke with him, children were grabbing him from behind or clambering onto his shoulders, from which height they would then tumble into his lap. They would laugh and shout and pull his ears or his beard, then try to squirm their way into the front of his robe. Far from seeking to rid himself of these intruders, Araki would join in their game, pinching the nose of one child, pulling the legs out from under another, and holding a third under his arm, all to the accompaniment of the delighted shrieks of the children.

Finally, taking notice of the ruckus, the mothers, Lord Araki's daughters, would appear and, apologizing, lead the children off, but it was quite clear that Araki seemed to think it a shame to put an end to such merriment. The daughters, as I have said, were all quite beautiful, but one in particular, I noticed as they tended to the children, was more beautiful than her sisters. Her bearing was very upright, like her mother's, and her manner was quiet and dignified. When I pointed her out to Organtino, he told me that she had a reputation as a great beauty not only here in her father's domain but in Kyoto as well.

During one of my visits to his castle, Araki spoke of his idea of happiness:

"The most wonderful thing in all the world," he said, "is a prosperous, lively household such as this. It is what I would wish for all my people, from the greatest to the least—that they should have a comfortable existence; if a home has warmth, cheer, and comfort, then nothing is lacking. To sleep in a warm bed, to relax like a dog without a care in the world, to be with friends, to live an average life without ambitions—that is the life for me. No ambitions . . . yes, that's exactly it—no ambitions. To sleep soundly as the common man. . . ." His speech trailed off almost wistfully.

I had been told that there was another side to Araki; I knew that in times past he had attacked Lord Wada, and that he was, even then, busily engaged in ingratiating himself with the Signore. Even so, the impression of the man that remains with me to this day—the impression of a man who longed to have done with ambition and to sleep the sleep of the humble—derives from this little speech that rose to his lips almost unconsciously from somewhere deep inside.

Organtino told me that Araki had once tried to make every single one of his subjects convert to a certain Buddhist sect, and had ordered that those who declined to do so be punished. Possibly he was the kind of man who, once convinced of the necessity of an action, will never rest until he has seen it accomplished regardless of any obstacles. Perhaps he was too self-willed and impatient to keep an idea to himself, seeking to force it on others however unreasonable it seemed.

I can attest to the shortness of his temper at least, having myself once witnessed a rather telling example. It was on the occasion of one of our visits to his residence. We were talking when one of the grandchildren tripped and fell over a pot that had been left in the garden, receiving a small cut on the forehead in the process. Looking out and seeing the child crying, Araki abruptly leapt up without a word and, jumping down into the garden in his bare feet, ran and gathered the child into his arms. There was something strangely agitated in his manner which proved, when he began to ask who had left the pot in the garden, to be in fact violent rage. I was reminded of the legendary temper of Cortés. Cortés, though, was generally acknowledged to have the ability to control its ferocity when the situation demanded, whereas Araki ended this little scene by becoming speechless with rage, his head wobbling quite uncontrollably.

The source of this fury was of course an exceedingly trivial matter, and it might seem hardly worth noting the incident at all when one considers his essentially virtuous nature. Nevertheless, the same qualities he displayed at that time—his quick temper and stubbornness—were eventually to lead to tragedy. And whenever I recall the later, more serious incident, it is to that lesser crisis at his castle that my mind returns.

On the twenty-fifth of December, fifteen seventy-six, the first Christmas was celebrated in the new church. Since I was no longer in Kyoto at the time, the details of the event are as I had them in a letter from Organtino. On that day, the long-awaited Father Joan Francisco had made his appearance, almost as if he had intended his arrival to coincide with the great feast. Standing, the people recited the Santa Maria in unison, tears streaming down their faces. As he presented his brother to the congregation—Organtino wrote—his own voice broke with emotion more than once. He felt, he said, that at that moment the first stage of his mission had finally come to an end. He recalled how he himself had first come to Frois's mission, and their experiences together in the early days, with nothing but the dilapidated house to call a church, and the world a place of fear and uncertainty, hunger and war. One of their predecessors—Father Vilela, perhaps—had painted a cross on a scrap of paper and tacked it to the wall; taking this symbol as their altar, they had dipped water with a wooden bowl and baptized believers.

By now those days were no more than a dream from the distant past, Organtino wrote. How gratifying, though, was the impression the church had made on the newly arrived young priest!

101

Francisco had said that the grandeur and beauty of the church had nearly caused him to forget that he was in Japan, and as one of those who had helped build it, Organtino felt the words to be hardly an exaggeration; in his view, the building of the church had actually helped swell the number of converts, and its magnificence would attract still more in the coming years. The mission, he said, was entering a new era that would be, as he put it, "a great hymn of praise to God." "Here in the heart of this small kingdom on these distant Oriental shores"—he concluded —"we are singing aloud the praises of the Lord." In my mind's eye I could see his round red cheeks wet with tears as he pondered these mysteries.

All the while I had been preoccupied with the building of the church, the great storm had raged on throughout the kingdom, with the Signore at its center as ever. In the autumn of the year in which the Takeda army was defeated, an insurrection of the Buddhist clergy in Echizen had also been put down, in less than a month. The Signore's immediate problems were thus reduced to confrontations with the Buddhist army ensconced in the fortress of Ishiyama in Osaka, and with the forces of Lord Mori, who were providing the Buddhists with assistance and supplies. The bonzes were calling for revenge against the Signore for his attacks on them at Nagashima and Echizen. With the defeat of the Takeda, however, they had lost the principal architect and leader of the plan to surround the Signore, while the Buddhists in other regions had already been crushed. The monks of Ishiyama therefore issued a particularly urgent appeal to Uesugi in the north, with the result that he was beginning to threaten the Signore from behind, thus preventing him from moving against Ishiyama immediately. Nevertheless, this pressure from the north bought the monks only a little respite, for presently the Signore's defenses to the north of the lake were complete, and he felt he could safely send his entire army to attack in the south without fear of retaliation from Uesugi. The single restriction on this plan was time: the campaign in the south could not be a protracted one if his defenses to the north were to remain effective. So it was that in the spring of fifteen seventy-six, just as we were merrily celebrating the ridgepole raising in Kyoto, an order was issued to the Signore's entire army that the Buddhist force at Ishiyama was to be destroyed in a single bold stroke.

The Signore's army was busy setting up fortresses and fortifications around the stronghold of Ishiyama, planning to cut off the supply lines from the sea being fed by the Mori. Slipping away from the construction site of the church, I set out to look for members of my arquebus corps who would no doubt be among the troops hastening to Osaka, but I had no success. I could only conclude that they had already passed beyond Kyoto.

I did, however, catch a glimpse of some of the musket troops, and noted that in the year or so since I parted company with them their numbers had increased substantially and their equipment had been simplified for better mobility. At a single order, they could switch formation from rank to file with an impression of great swiftness and agility. The pleasant days I'd spent with them at Gifu passed before my mind's eye once more. I already knew of the splendid showing they had made at Nagashino, and felt sure that in the face of such a fine force, Ishiyama too would probably submit before the month was out. No doubt the others in the crowd watching with me were thinking similar thoughts.

When May arrived, however, the reports of the attack reaching Kyoto were not reassuring. It seemed that the first wave sent against the castle had been fired upon by several thousand marksmen, and that the defenders had numbered more than ten thousand in all. Rank upon rank of the vanguard of the Signore's army—the pick of its troops, under the command of Akechi, Araki, and Matsunaga—had been cut down in the initial charge. The reports concluded that the Buddhists had been quick to switch their gun companies to the triple file method of firing used by the Signore at Nagashino, and also that they possessed a large number of highly accurate muskets and a formidable stock of powder and shot. Furthermore, they had erected wooden stockades around the castle; whenever the assault was particularly fierce, the marksmen would retreat behind these and, taking careful aim, mow down the ranks of the Signore's main force. This done, they would advance the stockades. On the first day, before the attack was many hours old, a number of the Signore's generals had lost their lives. Harada, Hanawa, Niwa, and others were among the dead. In fact, the tide of battle quickly seemed to turn in favor of the defenders, who mounted an assault of their own to threaten Akechi in the fortress of Tennoji.

The Signore himself had not been on hand for this first encounter, but as soon as he received word that his army was locked in mortal combat, he left Kyoto and headed for the lines with a hundred mounted attendants. He was well aware that the setbacks of these early hours could affect the morale of his troops, and he knew too that there could be more widespread repercussions for his strategy of keeping the armies of Uesugi and Mori in check while carrying out the attack on Ishiyama. Thus on the second day after his arrival in Osaka, he took personal command of the attacking forces.

Runners from the battlefield kept us informed of the progress of the campaign. The next day was hot and humid, the sky overcast. In the half-light of dawn, the Signore's army, in triple-rank formation, advanced on the south slope of Ishiyama. The western side of the fortress, we were given to understand, was protected by the sea, while on the other three sides deep moats had been dug and flooded with water. The castle itself had thick stone walls and earthen breastworks, tall wooden barricades, holes through which muskets could be fired, and watchtowers for surveying the area. Within the fortress were innumerable temples with quarters for the priests, and a whole town devoted to supplying their needs.

With its fierce independence and sense of self-sufficiency, this religious community was often compared with Sakai, and in trying to picture it to myself I recalled the orderly streets and crossroads of that port, so often called the Venice of Japan. Unlike Sakai, though, the town at Ishiyama had already twice repulsed attacks by the Signore's army, and—I reflected—would no doubt have benefited from those experiences to shore up any weakness in its defenses.

From first daylight until late dusk, the battle that day pitted gun against gun. The Signore himself ran crouching through the lines, designating targets for attack, ordering advances and retreats, redeploying his forces. From every part of the field shots rang out and clouds of white smoke drifted up. Cries could be heard from beyond a dense thicket that grew on the battlefield, and the shot raining on the dry earth of the embankments sent up showers of dust. Just as a company of Buddhist lance bearers was preparing to leap down from the embankment to attack, more than a hundred muskets barked within the thicket. Under this onslaught, one flank of the Signore's army began to crumble, and there was a dangerous moment when the whole line seemed on the verge of turning and running. Quickly, though, the Signore summoned a company of reinforcements to the rear of the lines. From time to time, shot raining down from the stockade would pin down the advance companies, and he would order a hasty retreat. Soon, thick smoke hung over the whole field, lifting momentarily from time to time to reveal glimpses of the action, then closing down again like a briefly drawn curtain. Here, men were seen running full tilt across the plain; there, a man was glimpsed bent backward by the force of a direct hit. Men were charging, crawling, standing to fire their muskets. . . .

Suddenly, a great body of Buddhist troops, their faces distorted with tension, fell upon one flank of the Signore's army. A furious yell arose, arms clashed noisily, spears and swords flashed, blood sprayed, horrifying cries rent the air. As one force bore down in attack, an equal force rose up to meet it. The earth trembled as though beneath the feet of thundering herds; the guns rang out; there was more furious shouting. Conch shells bellowed across the field as both armies rushed forward. Then the guns fired once more, and the shot whistled over the heads of officers and men as they lay on the ground. For a moment the battle would die down only, abruptly, to renew itself with even greater fury. In many places, the bodies already lay heaped one on the other.

Eventually, it became apparent that the Signore's army was in general retreat, with the Buddhists in close pursuit. Three thousand guns fired in unison, then, before the smoke had cleared, the second rank fired. It was in that burst that the Signore's right leg was grazed by shot. He fell in a hollow but, rolling over, managed to climb back to the rim. He said later that he felt little pain, that the sensation was more one of heaviness, literally as if a weight had been attached to his leg. He ordered the retainers who rallied around him to command the army to take refuge in the fortress of Tennoji, and they instantly set about obeying him, making their way through the heavy fire. Though the fighting was fierce, the lines held as the retreat was accomplished. It was nearly noon by the time the whole army had reached the fortress.

But the respite was short-lived, for no sooner had they got their second wind than the Signore ordered an attack on the eastern face of Ishiyama. They must close—he told his generals—thus depriving the Buddhists of any chance to use their deadly muskets.

In the afternoon, the fighting resolved itself into a series of bold charges. The Signore's troops were arrayed in two ranks. After the first had forced a way past the most hazardous ground, that is, the most vulnerable to musket fire, the second would launch its attack. Once the lines were directly engaged, it was impossible for the Ishiyama marksmen to fire into the fray, since their own troops were fighting there. Finally, the Signore's lines began to advance and the Buddhists to fall back. With the vindictiveness of a hunting dog that has at last managed to fix its teeth in the bear that wounded it, the Signore's army chased the great army of Buddhists to the very gates of the Ishiyama stronghold.

As darkness fell, however, the Signore's army, having barely managed to maintain the upper hand, once more retreated to the Tennoji fortress to lick its wounds. Runners came to the Signore from the other strongholds where his forces were quartered, and each reported a similar situation. The entire army had suffered heavily that day.

That evening in Tennoji, a conference to consider strategy was convened. The first item of discussion was the unforeseen and drastic increase in the enemy's strength. It was estimated that by now the defenders rather than the attackers had the numerical advantage. Moreover, where the Buddhists had erected stout fortresses, the Signore's own men were left standing unprotected on the plain. The situation was the reverse of that at Nagashima; there, the insurgents had had no guns, and their supply lines were cut. Now, their supply lines were being maintained by the powerful navy of the Mori, and the western access from the sea allowed for the continual replenishing of ammunition and provisions. The only bright spot in the first day's fighting was the relative success of the strategy the Signore had devised: once the deadly musket fire was crossed, the Buddhist army was relatively vulnerable. But it was already clear that this strategy would prove far too costly to continue. It was generally agreed that a more patient plan was called for. As he listened to the views of his generals, the Signore's face was pale and set, his gaze directed into the distance. He himself, however, said not a word. To those watching him, it appeared that some scheme was germinating deep within his mind. The following day, the battle had already reached a deadlock. The besieging army made no move to attack, the defenders held their breath and waited. Very occasionally, scouts of the opposing armies would encounter one another and skirmish on the edge of the thicket, and shouts would be heard in the camps, but for the most part an uneasy silence weighed heavily on the troops of both sides.

The hot sun beat down on the soldiers in the fortress. Blue-green lizards ran over the dry stones of the wall, and the golden eyes of a snake flashed as it slithered along the earthworks. From time to time a breeze blowing from the sea would set the trees atop the hill rustling, and the soldiers behind the walls would tense with anticipation. But the wind would die down again; by the middle of the day, the heat was so fierce that they were forced to seek some shaded spot to rest.

A month passed in much the same manner. The Signore returned temporarily to Azuchi to see to the construction of his *palazzo*, which was just getting under way. The project was one that could not be ignored, even in the midst of battle. We had thought our own plans for the church most ambitious, but the palace was to be on a different scale altogether, and it was to be built moreover in a great hurry. It was rumored in Kyoto that two or three thousand rocks, each the size of a house, were being brought to Azuchi.

At the height of that summer, however, a runner came to Azuchi with an urgent message saying that the Mori navy had arrived at Ishiyama. It consisted of nearly eight hundred ships and boats, all of which were now drawn up in a tight semicircle around Ishiyama castle in order to unload provisions. This eventuality had, of course, been foreseen ever since the beginning of the siege, but the next messenger brought news of an unforeseen and untoward nature. The Signore's navy—the same navy that had presented such a majestic sight at Nagashima—had been attacked by the guns and flaming arrows of the Mori navy, and all three hundred ships had been burned and sunk, with the loss of a great many officers and men.

Coming as it did on the heels of the unexpected setbacks at the outset of the siege of Ishiyama, this was a severe blow. But as you are aware, my friend, crises of this sort have a way of following each other. It was not long before still more messengers arrived at Azuchi with word of subtle indications in the movements of both the Uesugi in the north and the Mori in the west suggesting that they were conspiring to attack the Signore on two new fronts at once. Although the Signore had a fortress at Gifu, the defenses at Azuchi were still unfinished and hardly prepared to resist an onslaught from the northern army. Moreover, Ishiyama castle had an unlimited source of supplies and could withstand a siege virtually indefinitely; the one hope seemed to be a sudden, desperate attack on the fortress to settle the issue once and for all, but several thousand accurate muskets were a strong argument against such a plan.

No doubt the Signore felt a similarity between this dilemma and the one that had faced him some years earlier when he was surrounded in Kyoto. Arguably, however, conditions were even less favorable this time. On the earlier occasion, the Signore's troops had been buoyed up by the feeling of invulnerability that comes of never having tasted defeat. While earning the private condemnation of Lords Sakuma, Takayama, and Araki, the Signore's campaigns of devastation—the burning of the sacred mountain and the subjugation of Nagashima among them—were, all in all, rather good for the morale of his troops. In the present case, however, it was known to all that the Signore's navy had disappeared without a trace at the hands of a superior force, while Ishiyama had begun to seem almost impregnable. Morale in the Signore's ranks had ebbed; at times, even, there was an un-precedented whiff of fear.

On the day following the Feast of the Ascension, I set out for Azuchi. I went with Organtino's blessing, for it was quite clear to him that the fate of the church was inextricably linked with the Signore's fortunes in war.

Azuchi proved to be one vast construction site situated on a plain by the shore of the great freshwater lake. The plain was backed by three small hills rising on the horizon like the humps of a camel. The Signore's *palazzo* was being built on top of one of these. Everywhere were rows of colossal rocks and great piles of timber, gravel, paving stones, sand, and other supplies, with a small city of huts for the carpenters and laborers. The activity was quite overwhelming; men seemed to swarm over the earth like an army of ants. Some were cutting wood, others planing it or chiseling out joints. Groups of coolies were carrying off the finished lumber, or baskets of earth and sand. There were stonemasons, men leading pack horses, men pushing carts, men pulling ropes, and many others besides. The overseers and soldiers who stood watching were giving the workers vocal encouragement, and a general sense of organization and industry prevailed as work went ahead according to the plans being transmitted from the Signore.

I reached a wing of the yet unfinished *palazzo* just as the Signore was conferring there with several persons. He expressed pleasure at my visit, and said that he had, in fact, been intending to seek me out in Kyoto in the near future. Then he continued:

"The gentlemen assembled here are among the kingdom's leading manufacturers of firearms. They come, mostly, from Sakai and Kunitomo village. Today I have asked them to bring here the products not only of their own shops but of other towns and villages as well. We also have here a musket that was captured from the rebels at Ishiyama. As you may have surmised, the purpose of our little meeting here today is to determine whether one of these gentlemen has made this gun and sold it to my enemies. I will say quite frankly that, if that proves to be so, I will instantly have the head of the guilty man, and his factory, his village, and all the other villages round about will be put to the torch.

"Well then, let us see if we can find the brother of the Ishiyama musket among these. I should add that I have also sent investigators to the villages concerned to look into these matters, but I suspect they will learn nothing. That is why I am particularly glad to see you, my foreign friend—since you are so knowledgeable about this matter of making guns. I would be grateful if you would examine these muskets and arquebuses for signs of kinship with the Ishiyama gun."

When the Signore had finished, a heavy silence fell over the room. The gunmakers watched me closely as I examined their wares. It did not take me long to detect distinguishing characteristics in the guns of both Sakai and Kunitomo: the barrels, the shapes of the muzzles, the bores, the firing chambers, pan covers, powder bowls, triggers, and breeches. The guns from Kunitomo, for example, used a wheel lock in the firing mechanism—an idea no doubt borrowed from my own arquebus. This feature was conspicuously absent from the gun brought from Ishiyama. In form, it was more similar to those from Sakai, but the quality of the materials was far inferior in the captured gun. In sum, the musket from the Buddhist stronghold was more primitive in both concept and execution.

I shook my head. "There is no resemblance," I told the Signore. "This gun comes from a completely different source." A deep sigh of relief escaped the lips of several of the gunmakers.

"Well then," said an old man who sat among them, "it's just as I thought. It comes from Saiga."

"It does seem most likely...," another chimed in.

"So it does," agreed the Signore. "That is the only possible explanation." His gaze was fixed again, his pale brow twitching. No doubt he was already considering how to cut off this supply of arms to the Ishiyama fortress.

He had previously, I learned, made inquiries as to what places were capable of manufacturing several thousand guns in a short period of time, and had long been aware that Saiga in Kishu had turned against him and was cooperating with the Buddhists. He knew, too, that its guns had already been distributed to rebellious fiefs throughout the kingdom. However, it was only with the battle of Ishiyama that he realized that the capacity of the Saiga factories was in no way inferior to those of Sakai and Kunitomo. My little test only served to make this discovery all the clearer.

Perhaps because I was, by that time, quite familiar with the Signore's strategic thinking, I guessed intuitively that he would seek to fight his way out of his troubles by aiming first at this gun factory in Saiga. I wondered, however, how effective this would prove, since even if he managed to destroy Saiga, the Mori navy would still be able to supply Ishiyama. The present stock of guns in the fortress, even without the benefit of additional muskets, seemed adequate to withstand almost any attack. Thus I reasoned—as I was sure the Signore had himself—that the next logical step was to destroy the Mori navy. But what stroke of genius could accomplish such a formidable task? How was the Uesugi army to be held off in the meantime? And even if the right plan could be devised, would there be enough time to put it into effect?. . .

I remembered how I had racked my brains over the Signore's predicament as I stood on the watchtower of the *palazzo* at Gifu and sensed the approach of the Takeda forces. Hadn't he managed then, by a bold stroke, to save himself? No, I thought: it was, rather, a miracle that had occurred. Against all probability, the Takeda army had broken off its advance and receded like the tide. Shingen had died, suddenly and unexpectedly. But could one hope now for a second miracle? Lord Uesugi was, as far as I knew, in the best of health. I studied the Signore's face and found it strangely gloomy. Never had I seen him looking so forbidding, not even on the morning he had given orders for the slaughter at Nagashima. There was a grimness in his expression that struck dread in the heart.

Some time after this, as the construction of the church was drawing to a close, I again had occasion to be numbered among the Signore's advisers, being given the task of collaborating in the building of a warship adequately armored to withstand the guns of the Mori navy. I was also to work with an old gunsmith in making a cannon to be mounted on this ship. On the day I received these commissions from the Signore, I felt I had begun to understand what had made his face so dark and grim. It was neither anger nor despair, but a determination to overcome his dilemma by means of meticulous, patient, and farsighted planning. It was as if he were walking a tightrope—time—balancing himself by means of a tremendous effort of the will. The question was whether or not he would reach the other end of the rope. Or perhaps a different metaphor would be more apt: he was not, you see, simply walking a straight line, but was bringing together and delicately coordinating a thousand discrete movements like the works of the overly complex Venetian clock he had returned to Father Frois. Despite all the planning, who could say whether the cogs would mesh smoothly as theory was translated into recalcitrant reality? And what of the planner himself? Would he bear up until he had put in place the final wheel, the one that spelled out victory?... The grimness of the Signore's face had been due, I realized, to the extraordinary difficulty of the task he had determined to accomplish.

In order to begin work on the ship, I left Azuchi and headed for the sea at a place called Ise. The coastal region here was under the control of Lord Kuki, and I was going to Ise to join the navy that he had forged by unifying several pirate bands and that now comprised the bulk of the Signore's remaining strength at sea.

I had decided that we should pattern our ship after a square-rigged, three-masted caravel of the kind on which I had sailed on my first passage out of Lisbon. The ship that had carried me to the New World had been sheathed with steel plates rather like a knight in full armor.

The shipwrights showed me some of their handiwork, and I discovered several distinct differences from the caravel. There was, for example, nothing in the Japanese ships corresponding to a keel, nor anything like ribbing, the planks of the hull being simply fixed one on top of the other from the bottom to the deck. This technique interested me, and I decided that rather than attempt an exact copy of a caravel, it would be best to adapt what we could to the Japanese form, then armor the boat when it was completed. The shipwrights were lavish in their praise for the hull as I drew it for them, with its center keel and ribs to support the planks, and were more than eager to attempt a ship in that style. But they were steadfastly opposed to the idea of plating the body in steel. They said that such an addition would rob the ship of the speed necessary in battle. Satisfied that we were in agreement on fundamentals, I did not offer any objection at this point.

The drawings were made by the head shipwrights, and after I had made a few revisions they were studied by the entire company. We began to cut timber at the end of fifteen hundred and seventy-six. The report that the Signore's army had destroyed the town of Saiga came in the last days of the following February, by which time the hulls of some of the ships (we were in fact constructing six at once) had already been assembled and the decks were in place.

I next spent half a year in the company of the elderly gunsmith, working on the design and casting of a cannon and muskets to be mounted on our ships. This work presented a series of novel challenges, from the casting of such large barrels to the sizing of the shot and preparing of the powder. But the old man seemed to possess the gift of perfect intuition in such matters. He had, in fact, already experimented for his own purposes with the casting of large ordnance, but time was needed to enlarge his design and make some adjustments that would allow it to be mounted on a ship.

Occasionally, the Signore's grim countenance would rise up in my mind, at which times I felt a great impatience to have the work advance as quickly as possible. The feeling was perhaps most acute in August of that year, when we learned that Lord Matsunaga had betrayed the Signore and joined the rebels of Ishiyama. The major reasons for this act of treason were that fighting had been stalemated for a year and a half, and that it was increasingly apparent that Uesugi was moving to attack the Signore from the rear, so that private misgivings about the Signore's strategies and strength were giving rise to uneasiness and trepidation among his allies.

Fortunately, the Matsunaga affair as such was settled within two months, but no one doubted that it had done great damage to the Signore's cause. If the stalemate continued, a second and then a third Matsunaga would almost certainly make their appearance, and to avoid this possibility it was essential that something be done to rekindle the fighting spirit of the idle troops. No doubt the Signore's decision—taken almost as soon as Matsunaga had committed suicide—to cut off the Mori army's assault by moving his army to the west was based on such immediate considerations.

Such a move, however, was a gamble, to say the least, especially since Ishiyama castle was unlikely to capitulate while the Uesugi army was approaching from the north. The Signore's decision was, of course, influenced by the reports on our progress in equipping the Kuki navy, but it remained to be seen whether the ships would be completed on schedule, and then whether they would deliver the desired results. Nevertheless, it was the Signore's longstanding principle to take swift action, based on as accurate a judgment as possible, while others hesitated; and so it was that he swooped down on the front lines of his enemy to the west. In launching the attack, he entrusted the left flank along the coastlands to Hashiba and the highlands on the right flank to Akechi. The latter's advance through the mountains proved extremely difficult, but along the coast the Mori army's line yielded readily.

It was at the end of that year that we completed three cannons and brought them to Ise to make a test in the presence of the shipwrights. Our guns had been set up at a distance of five hundred paces from a small cabin; they roared, and it vanished in a cloud of fire and smoke. The shipwrights who witnessed this display were left speechless for a time. It had never occurred to them that there could be a cannon of such tremendous power, and it was this perhaps that convinced them that ships carrying such a weapon must themselves be built to withstand a similarly fierce attack. Thus it was that our three-masted Japanese caravels went to sea tightly armored in steel plates.

My work was far from finished, however, for it remained to mount the guns on the ships; train the crews in their firing; drill the sailors in handling the unfamiliar ships and performing the maneuvers necessary in firing mounted guns; develop a system of semaphore for signaling between the ships; and practice sailing in formation. My days, and often my nights, were extremely busy around this time, but whenever I wearied I spurred myself on by recalling the Signore's grim, pale countenance. It might seem that this man's fate should have been a matter of supreme indifference to a citizen of distant Italy such as myself. What reason had I to care if the Mori army gained the upper hand, or someone named Matsunaga turned traitor? Yet, strangely enough, I had a deep sympathy for the suffering the Signore's heart bore in silence. And it seems to me, my friend, that if there is any value at all in the trials of human life, it lies in the ability to feel another's burden as one's own. (You have no doubt divined that my feelings for Organtino came from much the same source. I could see how faithfully he bore his particular cross, and it was this steadfastness that had attached me to him in Goa.) The tenacity with which such men cling to their tasks may at times border on madness; but they cling, nevertheless. The self is lost in the task; all meaning is concentrated in bringing the thing, whatever it may be, to fruition. Some may see in this a kind of philosophy or a creed, some may call it pointless overconfidence, but the crucial thing is that the man is aware of the weight of his own burden and shoulders it bravely. And he himself chooses the load that he wills himself to bear to the end. The Signore, I was sure, had chosen, and his life was a continual wrestling with himself. Everything else was meaningless for him; the will to endure was a flame burning fiercely within. I wonder to this day what it was that he saw as he stared far away into space. I only know that when the storms blew on the coast of Ise, or when I was handling a boat heading into the high waves, or when the five thousand men of the Kuki navy put to sea at dawn in our new fleet, I felt an immense satisfaction. The creaking of the masts, the low moan of the wind, and the changing colors of the tides gave me a sense of life perpetually renewed.

After a fortnight at sea, we reached the area known as Kii, where we awaited the first encounter that would test our new fleet. The battle that ensued, however, was hardly worthy of the name, for it was like a great, invincible elephant trampling through brittle brush. The ships and boats of the enemy fleet sallied forth, bravely enough, from Kii Bay and headed toward our six ships, firing muskets and flaming arrows as they came. Without responding, we continued our orderly advance, still in formation. Their attack had no effect whatsoever on the sturdy armor of our hulls. Only when the enemy had thus been lured into the circle we formed was a red banner unfurled on the ship carrying Kuki himself. At this signal, a great broadside of musket fire belched forth from the six ships. Through a curtain of white spray, we could see the small boats shaking and lines of sailors collapsing one on the other. The musket fire continued without pause, while arrows dipped in oil and set alight were finding their mark on the decks of enemy ships already in the grip of panic. Then, as if the attack had not enough ferocity already, the great guns commenced their thunderous barrage. Their roar resounded across the waves. The sea was shrouded in flame and smoke, but we could just make out the sterns of the enemy ships as they turned to flee. Our three lead ships continued to fire their cannons. One well-aimed shot took off the entire aft section of a ship, which slipped beneath the waves in the space of a moment. Another ship was completely engulfed in flames, but refusing to sink went on blazing brightly on the surface of the sea.

Late in the afternoon, the Kuki navy resumed formation and set sail. As the sheets filled with a fair wind blowing into the straits between Osaka and the island known as Awaji, the triple-masted ships looked very much like those I had sailed in other seas. Later, when he saw the same ships at anchor in Sakai, Organtino was to comment on their resemblance to Portuguese caravels: until that moment, he said, he had had no idea what I had been doing for nearly a year at Ise.

The Kuki navy had successfully blocked the supply route to Ishiyama, and the fortress was at last isolated in a true siege. At the end of autumn, the entire Mori navy attempted to break the blockade, but was dealt a heavy blow by the six armored ships. This success in seizing control of the waters around Osaka came just at the moment of greatest need, for about the same time Hashiba and Akechi were encountering particularly stiff resistance from the Mori army, and both flanks had become embroiled in bitter fighting. The victory at sea gave the Signore just enough relief to avoid a final crisis. It was then, in a manner of speaking, that lightning struck the same place a second time, for Kenshin, commander of the Uesugi army advancing from the north, died suddenly just as Takeda Shingen had before him, thus ending the long winter of uncertainty that had held the Signore's land in its grip. And the first breath of this new spring had come with the appearance of our ships from the Sea of Kumano.

Nevertheless, the outcome of the siege of Ishiyama was still unclear, nor were matters helped by the fact that Lord Matsunaga's treason was not the last of those difficult days. As I have said, such things are bound to occur when a battle lies deadlocked. Months of waiting can lead the hearts of men astray, and others were tempted after Matsunaga: Araki, Takayama, and Nakagawa all changed their allegiance to the Buddhist side. Nor could all these rebellions be construed as mere opportunism, as a desire to back the winning side, for Lord Araki at least must have been plotting his move just as the Uesugi army withdrew to the north and the Kuki navy appeared off the coast.

It was, of course, rumored afterward that the principal cause of this rash of treachery was the suspicion that the Mori army would finally prove overwhelmingly superior. I cannot say with certainty whether or not this was in fact behind the rebellions of Matsunaga and Bessho, but in Araki's case I seriously doubt it. I prefer to believe that for him it was less a fear of being on the losing side than a long-held mistrust—bordering at times on abhorrence—of the Signore. Organtino (who was, as I have said, somewhat intimate with him) had often told me that Araki harbored such feelings, and he said later that, just prior to openly leaving the Signore's ranks, Araki had refused to obey his orders for an all-out onslaught, saying that he preferred to avoid such useless bloodshed. I recalled the earlier occasions, while the court was still in Gifu, when Araki and Sakuma had asked me what a man from a Christian country thought of the Signore's strategy of merciless annihilation. And I had wondered vaguely whether their misgivings might not some day develop into a direct confrontation, even though at the time I understood nothing of the factions that divided the court—and was not always able, even, to distinguish one lord from the other. Even at that early date, I had the distinct impression that a group of dissenters existed at court, and that the relative moderation and good-naturedness common to them naturally led to an interest in the Christian religion.

I had finished my work with the Kuki navy and returned for the time being to the splendid church in Kyoto when I first heard the news of Araki's defection. As often in those days, I was in a small room at the back of the church dismantling and cleaning my arquebus when one of the Japanese friars, pale as a ghost, rushed in with the news. Before being baptized by Frois, he had been a warrior from the fiefdom of Sanga. Then, some years after baptism, he had elected to take vows as a friar. As he explained what had happened, Organtino, who happened to be in the church at the time, cried out *"Impossible!"* Our surprise was still greater, however, at the friar's next revelation: Lord Takayama was expected to follow suit shortly.

"Dario (for the Japanese Christians refer to one another by their baptismal names) must feel a special sense of obligation to Lord Araki for making him castellan of Takatsuki castle." The friar, as a member of the noble *samurai* caste, was well up in the politics of the Gokinai area. "What is more," he continued, "his son Justo has further guaranteed his complicity by sending his own younger sister and child as hostages to Arioka castle, which is held by Araki."

I saw the blood suddenly drain from Organtino's round, boyish face. By the time the friar finished, he had turned completely white. He seemed about to say something, to raise his hands to gesture, but instead went suddenly limp and stood with a dazed look on his face, muttering again and again: "Justo . . . Dario . . . impossible . . . impossible. . . ."

We learned the very next day that the friar's prognostication was accurate: Takayama had indeed gone to Takatsuki castle to let his new sympathies be known. It is difficult to conceive the confusion this must have produced both at the siege of Ishiyama and along the battle lines with the Mori army.

I found myself trying to imagine the Signore's feelings. Was he simply in a rage? Or was he, above all, contemptuous of Araki's ingratitude? He might also, with good reason, be in a state of consternation, if not outright panic. Or perhaps he was simply despondent? In the end, however, it seemed to me that none of these was likely. The only image I could conjure up was of the Signore's gloomy countenance with its piercing gaze fixed on that same point in space. The face, in my mind's eye, bore no trace of either malice or rage. Nor, however, was there any sign of compassion or pity for his new enemies. If I were to name the quality I saw there, I should call it sorrow. The pale, sad visage was no longer merely gloomy, but desolate and lonely. Suddenly, it occurred to me that the Signore had loved Araki; and I seemed to hear the Signore's voice calling out from a great distance:

"Old man!" it said "Old man! Why did you turn your back on me? Did you think, perhaps, that I was displeased with you? I swear that I never was. On the contrary, you have been close to my heart ever since the time when you and Hosokawa drove off that ignorant, vain, and dangerous Kubo-sama. At that time, you came to meet me in Osaka, and I was delighted to consider both of you my friends—Hosokawa who had such strong ties with the court in Kyoto, and you, old man, with your influence in the Gokinai. I was too busy then chasing after my own ideals to look around me. But when I met the two of you—old Hosokawa, so refined, so like an affectionate father, and you, so dependable under your lively exterior—I realized how lonely my fight had been. In short, I was fond of you. Yes, old man, I liked you very much—your swarthy, wrinkled face, your kind, cheerful eyes, your stout, sturdy body that seemed to belong among the humbler ranks of men, your stubborn jaw ... yes, everything about you. Even your country ways, your short temper, and your stubborn streak pleased me. If you had talked to me, say, of the grandchildren you loved so much, I would have felt, for a moment at least, as though my own loneliness had been relieved.

"I know, old friend, that you consider me a heartless and cruel man. You think I would not understand talk of your darling grandchildren. And I won't deny that you had ample grounds for your view, for never once did I pardon any of those for whom you sought mercy. On the contrary, I invariably ordered my enemies hunted out and put to death to the last man. But you knew—for I told you myself on more than one occasion—that I had my reasons for this policy, the chief of them being that I was unwilling to mar the hallowed rites of battle with acts of kindness.

"Because I refused to sink to vulgar kindnesses, I have stood alone in an empty darkness, with none to whom I could turn. I stand there still—though not quite alone any more, for now and then in the blackness I see the souls of those who have died by my hand. They drift by me like wraiths, their eyes full of grievance, their hands reaching out for me, their voices crying low: 'Why did you not spare us?' How many of these spirits do you suppose visit me, old man, here in the darkness? And how do you suppose I answer them? I tell them that, given the chance to have them in my grasp again, I would not be satisfied with their death, but would shred them like rags until they were unable even to cry their miserable question. I would grind them in a mortar, so they might never again take even ghostly form. . . .

"The wind drives away the ghosts with a mournful wail, and I am left alone in the darkness, alone with the icy wind . . . I am left, enduring the bitter cold in that black void. Do you hear, old man? Sometimes this weakness you call kindness turns men into base creatures; knowing that, I will never permit myself to indulge it. It

122

can never be permitted, even if it means that someone is condemned to hang on a cross for a thousand, two thousand years without light or hope. My old friend, I am not seeking blood for its own sake. I seek one thing only: the will to attain the utmost possible to man, the will to human perfection. . . ."

You may think that I was amusing myself with idle fancies, but I do not believe that the Signore's true feelings were far from what I have imagined, for in the first days after news of this treachery was brought to Azuchi, the Signore dispatched Akechi and Hashiba, both intimates of Araki, to try to persuade him to change his mind. Even those who whispered of these doings in Kyoto could hardly believe that such extraordinary efforts would have been made to regain Araki's cooperation if the Signore's only concern were to restore order to his forces. They looked for reasons for the Signore's hesitation to retaliate. Some maintained that had Araki shown the least inclination to submit, he would instantly have obtained the Signore's pardon—but that a pardon under such circumstances would be untrustworthy, and that Araki would have felt the Signore's ire at some later date.

I believe they were overly suspicious, as the case of Takayama and his son shows. With Takayama, it was Organtino who was selected as mediator—a choice that immediately started a rumor that the Signore had threatened to cut off all relations with the Christians if Takayama did not return to the fold. To my knowledge there was never any truth to this rumor. If such a possibility was ever mentioned, it was probably a mere conjecture made by the wise and perceptive Takayama himself, who might have feared that the sending of Organtino portended something of the kind. And if Takayama had asked the eminently practical Organtino whether such a thing were possible, he might well have responded that it was not beyond imagining. Some conversation such as this might well have been the source of the rumors.

Whatever went on between them, Organtino did in fact persuade Takayama to return to the Signore—who, far from punishing him, actually praised his courage and resolve. Toward the father also—Dario—the Signore adopted a most lenient attitude. One could only conclude that he was making a sincere effort to regain the hearts of those who had turned against him. Perhaps even he could not bring himself simply to write them off as traitors. Perhaps the loneliness would have been unbearable. To the last, I believe, his one wish was to make them understand his true intentions.

I remember how, one day when Organtino and I had come to Azuchi at the Signore's request, we found him standing at a window of the still unfinished palace, looking out over the lake at the patterns traced on its surface by the wind, and how I felt that in the icy waves churning the lake he saw a reflection of his own cold and troubled human ties.

It was not long thereafter that the entire household of Araki met its end in a single day, amid scenes that I fear, my friend, I will not soon forget. When Araki himself fled Arioka *castello* for the fortress at Amagasaki, the Signore took prisoner all those who had been left behind and ordered that all of them, even the humblest servants, be put to death immediately.

It was a cold morning in December when we arrived at Shichihonmatsu near Amagasaki castle. The sky was clear except for a faint trace of cloud high up in the heavens, and a chill, sharp wind off the sea cut through our clothing. A crowd of people from the surrounding villages had already collected outside the hastily erected barrier around the execution site, and stories were being traded of the misfortunes that had befallen all those in any way linked to Araki. A certain man was condemned because he had written a letter to his son who was confined with his master in Amagasaki castle. Another had pleaded that his wife might be spared, only to be sentenced to die with her. A woman had written a letter saying that she would be happy to die for her husband's sake.

The winter sun had just risen and a weak, ruddy light fell over the frost-covered earth. A murmur started a short distance from the fence and ran through the crowd to the spot where we were standing. One hundred and twenty-two women dressed in white *quimono*s were filing toward us with their hands tied behind their backs, surrounded by soldiers whose black uniforms seemed especially sinister against the white robes. Many of the doomed women were Christians who had been known to Organtino at the church in Kyoto, and as they passed he knelt on the ground and prayed.

Their faces betrayed only a peaceful melancholy, and those who had come to witness their execution could not but mark their bravery. Some of the onlookers were themselves weeping bitterly. Organtino held out a cross toward the women, and one of them, catching sight of his familiar face, bowed slightly. One after the other, the women were bound to tall stakes which the soldiers then set up in the center of the open field. A fierce wind had been blowing all the while, yet a strange quiet prevailed on the execution ground as though the pillars had always been there, with the edges of the white kimonos curling in the wind. A long time seemed to pass.

Suddenly, a sharp thud sounded from a *taiko* drum, and I looked up just as the musket company fired on the women hanging there. There was a red flash, then smoke. As the roar of the blast reached my ears, the white robes were flecked with black, then, instantly, splashed with red. Heads nodded forward on several of the pillars—the ones where death came easily, kindly— but from the rest, indescribable screams showered down upon us. All bloodied, they flung back their heads, writhing and shrieking in pain. Then, a second group of soldiers ran toward the women with lances raised. As the flashing blades did their grim work, most of the screams were extinguished like sputtering flames, but a few of the women, like blind, wounded beasts, thrashed and wailed all the more as the soldiers wielded their lances. It was all we could do to remain still.

Several days later, we heard that more than five hundred of the lower-ranking *samurais* and servants, together with their women, had been herded into four houses piled about with dry grass and kindling. These were then set ablaze and every last soul was burned alive. It was said that though the flames were fanned to a terrible height by the gale then blowing, the voices of those within could be heard above the wind and the roar of the fire, pleading for mercy. Even after the houses had been reduced to charred ruins, voices still escaped from the chaos of burned bodies that continued to wriggle like maggots in the glowing mass.

Yet even among these fearsome events, the one I find most difficult to put from my mind is the execution of Araki's beautiful daughters and their children, which took place on the riverbed at the spot known as Rokujo in Kyoto. Before the execution, they were paraded in open carts through the streets of the city, where I chanced to catch a glimpse of them. In the second cart rode the remarkably beautiful daughter whom I have mentioned before. Just as on the day we saw her at Araki's castle, she knelt calmly, her body erect; all who beheld her were awed by her beauty and her noble melancholy.

I had not the heart to go to Rokujo that day, and can only relay to you the account of their death given me by one of the Christians who was present. He was especially insistent on one point: that to the end these women and children never once lost the calm and dignity they had shown in the carts.

"The children," he said, "met death with the same composure. When they reached the spot by the river, they asked a soldier if they were to die in that place, and on hearing the answer, knelt in a line and waited peacefully as if they had no idea what was about to happen. When the time came, they stretched their little necks forward as if it were the simplest, most natural thing. May God receive their souls!"

The same little children who had once wrapped themselves around Araki's shoulders as he talked with us were no doubt among this group, and it impressed me deeply that children raised in such freedom should have died in a way befitting the off-spring of noble warriors.

The slaughter was over; but it had not, I suspected, achieved its desired effect. The sense of isolation and loneliness visited upon the Signore by Araki's treason could surely never be assuaged, the void left by the departure of this one friend never filled. Though he might pursue Araki to the ends of the earth, though he might crucify or behead his entire household, though he might im-molate all his retainers, nothing in the end could relieve the desolation.

I have told you before, my friend, how the Signore was well disposed toward Frois and liked to jest with Organtino. Further-more, I will have occasion to describe for you hereafter the Signore's very real affection for the Visitor-General to the mis-sion, one Alessandro Valignano, who arrived somewhat later. And I have told you why, as I understood matters, he was so well-disposed toward these men. He recognized in them, it seems to me, an extraordinary singleness of purpose, a willingness to go any distance, take any risk, for the sake of their God. He was par-ticularly pleased with them in that their trials had been so severe—giving sermons in a dilapidated old house, tending the sick, sharing their meager rations with the poor, rescuing women and children from slavery at great risk to their own persons. He saw a parallel between their discipline and suffering and his own ruthlessness both on the field of battle and off. Occasionally, I heard him refer to the padres as the "masters" of Christianity—

127

by which I am quite certain he implied that they gave themselves as wholly to service and charity as he gave himself to slaughter and victory.

Considering such matters, I found myself once again imagining the rebuke the Signore might, in his heart, have addressed to his faithless friend:

"The whole point, my dear Araki, is to be utterly consistent. You abhor my mercilessness in battle, but—I tell you truly— anything you do, if you do it not perfectly, is worse than meaningless. What meaning has mercy in the midst of carnage? Let me remind you of an event that occurred some years ago; you too will no doubt recall it. We were riding back to Omi together when we came upon a blind cripple who had taken shelter from the rain among the roots of a tree by the side of the road. I do not even remember from which campaign we were returning, but I will never forget how I was struck by that pitiful sight. And do not think, old man, that the look on your face escaped me when I gave the cripple twenty bolts of cotton. Later, I heard, you recounted the incident with the comment 'If only the Signore showed similar mercy in battle, his name would resound through the ages. . . .' But that is where your understanding is weak. For, you see, my pity for that poor man and my mercilessness in battle are one and the same thing! No doubt you fail to see, my old friend, that the only mercy in battle is to be merciless!"

More of my apocryphal imaginings? Perhaps. Yet something of the sort must surely have been in the Signore's head. If not, how is one to explain what happened next?

The siege of Ishiyama had barely ended—in the Signore's favor—when, without warning, one of the commanders of the victorious army, the scholarly Lord Sakuma, was banished. The sentence sent a great shock through the rest of the army, and it was generally felt that a great injustice had been done a man who by rights should be sharing in the spoils of a victory he had fought so long to secure. The reason given for the harsh punishment was, if accounts are correct, scarcely comprehensible: Sakuma, it seemed, was banished for his humanity and restraint in the final phase of the battle. The edict announcing his sentence, a document said to have been written in the Signore's own hand, contained nineteen clauses, one of which read:

> The way of the warrior is not that of others. In a battle such as the siege of Ishiyama, it is incumbent on the commanders—for their sake and for mine—to choose the most opportune moment, then attack with all they have. In this manner, the troops are spared prolonged hardship and struggle. It is the only rational course. But you, with your persistent reluctance and hesitation, have followed a course that can only be judged as thoughtless and unmanly.

You must not suppose, however, that these tumultuous events had any great visible effect on the Signore's everyday life. If anything, he became rather more austere and methodical than before. His hour for rising and retiring never varied, whether he was at home or in Kyoto or on the battlefield, and his schedule during the day was extremely regular. Before breakfast he went for a ride, and each subsequent activity was carried out with a diligence and care more typical in bankers and ministers of finance than in great lords. During its appointed period, he would do whatever he was supposed to do with apparently unflagging interest. Yet no matter how absorbed he might be in the activity at hand, once the designated time was up he would simply stop and move on, with no visible sign of regret.

I knew that my father and his friends in Genoa demonstrated a single-minded diligence in their daily lives that was not, on the surface, unlike the Signore's; and I was also acquainted with the bleak, vulgar utilitarianism that underlay that diligence. Yet compared with the lives of the conquistadors under whom I had

129

served in Nuova Spagna, or of the mercenaries in the Molucca Islands—lives ruled by chance and caprice, taken up with jealousy and vanity, easy prey to the honeyed words of underlings—the Signore's steadfast respect for his own principles and his willful deafness to the capricious, unreliable call of feeling seemed emininently worthy of respect.

The man who chose such a path risked a fearful loneliness, and the Signore's isolation must have been still more palpable once he had finally eluded the dangers besetting him and, with the sacking of Ishiyama, become, in name and deed, the Supreme Ruler under Heaven. The retainers who waited on his person, never bold, became all the more timid, flitting about him cautiously, waiting on his every whim, while the Signore, for his part, grew less and less inclined to merriment and jest.

It was clear that the sense of isolation began to weigh even more heavily on his heart following the banishment of Sakuma. But he was not the sort to wander out among men to seek comfort and companionship. If anything, his daily routine became, as I have said, even more rigorous, his conversation with his attendants more restrained. Not for a moment, it seemed, did he allow the chilly distance between himself and his court to lessen. Not a few of his vassals interpreted this new coolness as a sign of suspicion spawned by the treason of Araki and his mistrust of Sakuma. This view was particularly common among the members of the third faction.

Yet I hasten to add that none of these changes in the Signore were evident in his dealings with us. Toward us, his amicability, his childlike frankness, his curiosity, and his trusting nature— qualities best known, perhaps, to Organtino and myself—became if anything all the more evident after these incidents. As I have said, the Signore seemed to enjoy jests and humorous stories, and he was most decidedly not a somber, reticent man. So it was natural, perhaps, that when relations with his vassals grew stilted and he found himself more isolated than before, this lively, sociable, even humorous self came out more strongly than ever in our company. The vassals, in general, attributed this redoubled good will to Organtino's achievement in obtaining Takayama's retraction, while others said it was a further sign of the Signore's hatred for the bonzes. Perhaps so. But I suspect that such causes alone could not adequately have explained the effect—namely, the Signore's great kindness toward us, a kindness that I have only just begun to describe.

It was midsummer of fifteen eighty when Organtino and I paid a visit to the Signore in Azuchi to offer our congratulations on the completion of the new *palazzo*. The successful assault on Ishiyama that spring meant that the Signore's only remaining enemy was the Mori army in the west. The Takeda had yet to recover from the blow dealt them at Nagashino, so the Signore had sent the greater part of his army against the Mori. Once more, the flank along the sea was led by his favorite, Hashiba, and that in the mountains by Akechi.

Though this campaign was hardly at that point an unqualified success—the Mori had established clusters of fortresses along the frontiers and were putting up a disheartening degree of resistance—still, the overall situation had changed remarkably in the Signore's favor. The alliance that had formed to attack him from all sides had been smashed, and the only factor that defied exact prediction was the length of time it would take the Takeda to recover. Though it would not do to underestimate the strength this powerful domain had accumulated over the years, it seemed safe to say that for the time being it offered no real threat. Four dangerous fronts had been reduced to one: the Mori.

Thinking about it now, I am struck again by the genius that conceived such a broad strategy, that juggled several campaigns at once, meshing them skillfully together into a single force. Each element—our fleet of armored ships, for example—was no more than a single cogwheel in the mechanism of this giant Venetian clock, and while each wheel turned in an apparently independent movement, the whole worked together in admirable harmony. Seen in this way, even the siege of Ishiyama was not a simple clash of opposing forces but one piece in a much grander strategy.

As we made our way along the highway to Azuchi, I told Organtino how struck I was by the breadth of the Signore's vision. In retrospect, perhaps, it was only logical that he should have first sought to create difficulties for the fortress by attacking the source of its arms at Saiga, then built an invincible navy to cut off the supply routes themselves. Nevertheless, to devise such a slowly unfolding plan in the midst of such a crisis bespoke a lofty perspective and an almost superhuman patience. What discernment, indeed, to perceive the relation between such disparate activities as the designing of a ship's cannon and the siege of a fortress! Even though fortune, whether for good or evil, undoubtedly plays a role in a man's life, in an existence as exquisitely planned as this there was little room for anything but the orderly advance of reason.

Having been present in the Signore's camp when a messenger brought secret word of the death of the commander of the Uesugi army, I was privy to a demonstration of how little store the Signore in fact set by luck. One might have expected news of the death of a dangerous enemy to gladden his heart, still bedeviled as he was by this constant threat from the north. In fact, he listened to the report with a look of profound sadness. I doubt that it occurred to the Signore at that moment to consider the repercussions for his strategy. The death was a disappointment, the loss of a noble and worthy man. Such simple feeling occasioned his look of melancholy, a look utterly remote from vulgar considerations of personal advantage.

Most people seemed to consider the construction of the *palaz-*

zo at Azuchi as a means of vaunting the Signore's dominion over the land. But here too I think the notion mistaken. Though one might imagine the kings of the ancient Orient displaying their might with great buildings, it was quite inconceivable in a man like the Signore. I would remind you (as I might have reminded them) that he did not build Azuchi to celebrate his own greatness in conquering Ishiyama; he built it in the midst of the hard fight for Ishiyama, thereby putting a considerable strain on his resources—the reason being, it seems, that according to the Signore's principles the construction of Azuchi had equal priority with the destruction of Ishiyama. For administrative and strategic reasons, and also perhaps in a broader political sense, it was necessary to build a palace at Azuchi. Vanity, ostentation, and conceit had almost no place in his calculated political progression. In the arena of power play, Azuchi castle was just one force among others, one that was conceived with cool deliberation. . . . Such, in brief, were the things Organtino and I discussed as we journeyed on toward that castle.

Some time after noon on the day after our departure from the capital, it came into view. Though we had not been to Azuchi for some time, I had already been told, by members of the congregation, of the magnificent exterior and lavish interior fittings of the finished palace. Even so, the building now rising before us surpassed all their descriptions. Seen from afar, the *palazzo* sparkled like an enormous sapphire perched atop a hill. The color, we soon realized, came from the blue tiles covering the roofs of the pagoda-like tower that rose above the castle itself. Shining white walls ran around the perimeter. At the foot of the hill, where the construction site had been, the houses of the Signore's vassals and soldiers lined the streets of the new city, surrounded by a stone wall on top of which was a white parapet.

A deep canal had been dug to the hill from an inlet on the lake, and anchored in it were a number of ships reserved for quick passage to the capital. Along the streets by the canal stood boathouses, granaries, and other storehouses. In the same neighborhood were inns and markets, and the remoter of the houses for retainers.

Beyond the canal was the quarter designated for merchants and other commoners. Though the markets there were crowded and the streets bustled with activity, the area as yet was a town in name only. Many of the houses were but half finished and the land, though carefully laid out in neat blocks, was still dotted with fields and rice paddies and groves of trees. Nevertheless, buildings were going up everywhere; plaster for walls was being mixed, and carpenters were cutting lumber and planing boards.

Several hundred coolies were employed filling in the land along the shore of the lake. They loaded earth and sand dug from the hill into baskets and bamboo hampers, then, hoisting them on their shoulders, trudged off toward the lake in endless, regular files. Construction was also progressing on the great Azuchi highway—a wide avenue of hard-packed earth with willows and pines planted along both sides.

Dense undergrowth grew on the lower slopes of the castle hill. The palace rose beyond, and above it towered a magnificent seven-story keep, the eaves of each story covered with blue tiles. The windows looking out at us from the castle were finished in black lacquer with gold decorations. The ramparts had been formed by carefully fitting together enormous stones; above them, crenelated castle walls, pierced with slits for firing from, drew a dazzling white outline about the Signore's *palazzo*. The castle's stately presence seemed to shed a calm over the hill, disturbed only by the occasional breeze from the lake rustling the bushes on the slope.

We arrived in Azuchi not long after the fortress at Ishiyama had surrendered and been razed, and the victory had further increased the number of people who came to see the castle. As we approached the lower gate on horseback, the crowds parted to let us pass. Some merely stared in surprise, others pointed and shouted, while others again burst out laughing. But everyone was clearly startled at the sight of foreigners coming to visit the just finished castle.

Access to the castle gate consisted of nearly three hundred steps winding up through the great stones of the ramparts. The Christian *samurai* who had come to greet us pointed out several of the most colossal stones, explaining that four or five thousand men had been pressed into service to drag them up the mountain.

"I did not see the incident myself, but I am told that during construction a stone slipped and fell, so that more than one hundred men were crushed to death." The speaker glanced about as if looking for traces of the accident in the stones.

The outer castle gateway was furnished with a thick, heavy door studded with black nail covers. Next to the gateway, a watchtower had been built to provide a clear view of anyone standing outside. The watchtower and gateway were covered with beautiful blue tiles, and the decoration on the headtiles was finished with gold leaf. The walls were done in white plaster and the windows in them were fitted with black iron bars. There were also lines of gun holes in the wall so that the space uncovered by the other defenses could be protected as well. All these features were designed so that the outer walls could be quickly converted into a fortress in time of war. The genius at work was apparent even to one normally as unconcerned with such things as Organtino, who asked me in an undertone about what we had seen.

We passed through this outer gate, then the castle gate itself, and suddenly the tower was looming directly, almost menacingly, over us. It was surrounded by numerous lesser buildings, beyond which were storehouses for provisions and immaculately kept stables. Further on still, and enclosed by yet another thick wall, were the armories, though we learned this only later when we were taken on a tour of the inner castle.

As we came into the entrance hall of the *palazzo*, I marveled at the sumptuous decorations. There were great pillars of red lacquer embellished with gold, and sliding doors and screens decorated with paintings of flowers and birds done on gold leaf. The ceiling was divided into sections by a latticework of black lacquer with exquisite gold fittings. When I had visited the site three years earlier, the outer shell of the building was mostly finished, but work on the interior had not been started. Thus the feeling I had now was of seeing an altogether different place. We passed through countless rooms both large and small, each fitted with partitions speckled with gold and each splendidly decorated in a different scheme of colors. Some were subdued and elegant, others were laden with extravagant color, others again had a stately simplicity.

Organtino, Lorenzo, and I were ushered through many such rooms until we came at last to a hall looking out on a bright garden. The sky was reflected in a pond that lay about a lovely green hillock. A grove of trees stood nearby and beyond the knoll the blue-tiled roof of another building, apparently one of the bastions, could just be seen. We seated ourselves as bidden, and presently the Signore entered from the corridor attended by a group of young warriors. He wore *hakama* trousers over a linen *quimono*, as though he had just returned from the riding grounds. The pale, oval face with the piercing eyes and firm features was the same as ever, but the nervous expression and disturbing twitch of his brow were almost imperceptible that day. For several years past I had been familiar only with the gloom that care had chiseled on the Signore's face, and this sudden show of good spirits came like a clear sky after a long season of rains.

"Well, does my palace meet with your approval?" With one of

his rare smiles, he glanced around as if to gesture at the ceiling and the painted doors. We admitted that we were quite dazzled.

"Such a magnificent castle is more than the equal of the grandest palaces of Europe," Organtino offered.

"The equal of the palaces of Europe?" the Signore echoed, chuckling with satisfaction. "If that is so, then be good enough to inform the people of Europe that a new castle has been built at Azuchi."

"We will most certainly do so. We will convey word of this palace along with details of the Signore's continuing good favor toward us."

Organtino, the Signore replied in effect, might say what he pleased about his other activities, but he would be most gratified if he would write about the palace. "If you think it advisable, we might even have drawings made to accompany the report," the Signore added.

He then personally guided us, floor by floor, through every nook and cranny of the donjon. Beside the decorations, we were struck by the sheer size of the rooms, their complex arrangement, and their seemingly endless number.

"Yours is indeed an enormous palace," said Organtino. "We have walked a great distance, but have not once retraced our steps."

The Signore laughed again. "Just so! I myself often lose my way. That is why we have varied the decorations from room to room and placed images of the Buddha as markers."

The windows of the room in which we were standing commanded a view of boats coming and going on the blue lake, and of the flat expanse of open country dotted with hills resembling islands. A pale gray line of mountains was barely visible in the distance. The pillars in the room were lacquered black with gold ornament. Each square of the lattice ceiling contained a picture, and an old man who had served as construction supervisor explained to us the significance of these and the other paintings at the various levels of the tower. He pointed out the great variety of themes, ranging from landscapes, birds, animals, trees, and plants to Buddhist figures and classical Chinese allegories. As one climbed to the higher floors, he explained, the subject matter changed from the realistic and representational to more instructive and edifying themes.

When we reached the fifth level, the old man said:

"Please notice that on this floor, already, there are no longer any flowers or birds, no scenic views, no plants or animals. All are scenes depicting the life of the Buddha."

"Why are the pictures arranged in this manner?" I asked the old man.

"Perhaps these Christian gentlemen"—he turned and looked back at Organtino and Lorenzo—"would be better qualified to explain here, but the plan was to place the images most directly concerned with the human soul in the rooms closest to heaven."

The Signore listened to this speech with an air of satisfaction. The old man had been present on past occasions when the Signore had questioned Organtino about the existence of God and the soul.

Thus we arrived at the last and uppermost chamber, from which the whole castle, in all its newborn beauty, was visible in one sweeping view, knitted together in its length and breadth by the deep blue tile roofs and circled around by the green bushes on the slopes of Azuchi hill. The area cleared at the base of the hill for the town was a whitish gash in the plain of green. The people gathered in the markets, the boats being towed in the inlet, and the workers at the construction sites were all no bigger than ants.

"A wondrous view! Truly I have never seen a castle built on such a grand scale. From here one can see that the construction is progressing rapidly and that the city will soon be a fitting capital for your realm." As Organtino looked down from the window, he seemed once more to be the simple peasant child from the hills of Italy. It was this same simplicity, perhaps, that attracted the Signore to him.

"Signore—" He placed himself before the great lord with head slightly bowed. "I have an earnest request to make of you. I confess that I have long hoped for your permission to erect a Christian church in the city of Azuchi. If we were able to build a great church in the center of the realm, your lordship's fame would surely spread not just to the Christians of the kingdom of Japan, but to distant Goa, to Macao, and even to Europe."

The Signore pondered for a moment, apparently weighing the implications of this sudden petition.

"Well," he said at last, "in practice, I would not forbid it. You can see for yourself that we are building a great city here at Azuchi. Provided the church you propose was in every sense superior to the one in Kyoto, it would certainly be a worthy addition. Let us first select a suitable location, and I will furnish you with sufficient land. Where do you suppose would be the best spot?" He pointed out the window by which Organtino had been standing. "Nearer to the mountain, or to the lake? I will have the matter looked into at once."

Even as he descended the lacquered staircase, the Signore turned to Lorenzo to ask, "Does one build a church on the heights or by the shore?"

All day until sunset we were shown about the palace, the Signore, in high spirits, guiding us each step of the way. I cannot record at length all the details of that grand and opulent building. All I can say is that the construction of Azuchi castle required the assembled talents of the master craftsmen—architects, carpenters, carvers, joiners, painters, stonemasons, and artisans—of the capital, Gifu, and Owari. Their skills were brought to bear on every last detail; I noticed one especially striking example of this in a hall decorated with a painting of cranes by a pool of water. Many of the rooms had beautifully carved lintels over the doors, but in this particular room the lintel had an openwork scene showing a pine grove, rocks, and a stream, and, beyond the grove, a carved representation of Azuchi castle itself, the work of such delicacy that each story of the great keep could be clearly distinguished. On many of these lintels the carvings had been skillfully painted to enhance the effect.

While waiting for word from the Signore, we passed several days in Azuchi, during which we learned something of the town. From the base of the southern slope of the fortress, the city spread south and east to the shore of the lake. The streets were wide and precisely laid out, and workers cleaned them every morning and evening. There were markets, it seemed, at every turn: at the entrances to the harbor, by the canal, and in the main thoroughfare. Pleasant-looking inns and other, cheaper lodging houses lined the streets. Messengers from Kyoto and other cities, from the greater and lesser fortresses, hastened along the highway at all hours, urging their horses on to the castle at the top of the hill. *Samurais* who were off duty mingled with men and women who had come for a look at the new capital, and the streets were always crowded. Heavily laden pack horses and porters pressed through this throng on their way to and from the castle, bringing gifts for the Signore from every corner of the land, and a whole menagerie of living creatures as well: monkeys, parrots, dogs, horses, and other beasts of all kinds.

Organtino and Lorenzo took advantage of their few moments of leisure to visit the Christians who had already settled in Azuchi and tell them how permission had been granted to build a church in the city; they also, as was their wont, immediately set about preaching on the street corners of the town. Meanwhile, I went to see the men of the arquebus corps I had trained in Gifu. From these, I had an account of the fall of the fortress at Ishiyama, the resistance of the insurgents that continued thereafter, and the great fire that at last reduced the castle to ashes. Among these soldiers were some who had served in the navy under Lord Kuki, and as the saké was passed around, they struck up the songs they had sung as they rowed their ships to sea.

Barely three days had passed in this manner when a messenger came with a letter for Organtino from the Signore:

"I was gratified that you came this long way to see the new palace. As for the matter of the building site for the church that we discussed on the occasion of your visit, there stands in the center of the city a temple of the Tendai Buddhist sect. I would have no objection whatsoever to demolishing that temple, and nothing would please me better than to have the Christian church built on that site. If the location does not appeal to you, do not hesitate to say so. I feel, however, that this proposal would settle the matter most satisfactorily."

We set off immediately to see the temple, and with us went a number of the local Christian leaders. While recognizing that temples were often located in the center of town, and that such a location might well be considered most advantageous, Organtino was of the opinion that the site was too distant from the palace. He would prefer, he said, to build the church closer to the castle, as a sign of the Signore's patronage.

"It seems to me," he said to Lorenzo, "that there is no need to go so far as to tear down the churches of other faiths in order to prove that the Christian church in Azuchi has been officially sanctioned."

"I fully agree. I too have been thinking that it would be best to build the church near the hill, in the shadow of the castle if possible," the old man said, blinking his nearly sightless eyes.

At this, one of the Christians who had come with us put in a word:

"We also feel that such a thing would be most desirable. However, is is common knowledge that buildings with any sort of religious purpose are strictly forbidden in the vicinity of the castle. How then do you propose to build a church there?"

"There is no cause for worry," replied Organtino. "The Signore has promised to do everything in his power to grant our requests."

He looked in my direction as if to confirm my assent. Perhaps he was thinking of the service he had performed for the Signore in persuading Takayama to reverse his defection.

It had, indeed, been a service of considerable importance, for the outcome of the campaign against Ishiyama had virtually hung on Takayama's decision. The return of his troops to the Signore's lines had been every bit as important as the subsequent defeat of the Mori navy by the Kuki ships, and more than one of the chief vassals and advisers had spoken to me of the Signore's gratitude toward the father. If Father Frois or Father Organtino should come calling while they themselves were with the Signore—they told me—he would promptly drop everything, have them shown in, and in front of his generals and advisers launch into a debate on such topics as the existence of God or the immortality of the soul. On other occasions, he would have his attendants bring in a globe he had received from the Jesuits, and would question them about the route from Portugal to his own shores, or about the customs, geography, climate, and other particulars of the lands through which one passed on the way. The Signore was especially fond of this globe; he would often have it produced when I was present, when he would lead the talk around to geography, navigation, or astronomy, or to the customs of the people of Nuova Spagna, the subjugation of native peoples in colonies, and the like.

One of the Signere's advisors told me that once, when he was engaged in debate with Organtino and the other Christians, those waiting in the corridor had heard him exclaim in a very loud voice:

"I concede! You have bested me!"

His voice, by nature high-pitched and somewhat shrill, had been raised to a fearsome pitch by excitement; never had his tone betrayed such emotion as on that day. The occasion, as best I could determine, was one on which the clever old Lorenzo succeeded in demonstrating the immortality of the soul through logical argument; though it could well have been some other thing altogether. Either way, it was clear that the Signore was particularly fond of these discussions with Frois, Organtino, and company. Whenever the talk grew particularly heated, he would lean forward eagerly to press a point or listen to what was being said. A favorite phrase he would mutter at such times, folding his arms and staring straight ahead in silence as if holding a colloquy with himself, was: "Yes, that is most reasonable." He reserved such enthusiastic interest, though, exclusively for topics about which he might make this almost automatic comment—topics, that is, that were amenable to reasoned thought. His fondness for the globe, for the arts of gunsmithing and fortification, and for all the natural sciences was in fact due to their inherent "reasonableness." I remember in particular the earnest look on his face as he listened to me discussing, as best I was able, the mechanics of the solar and lunar eclipses. He sat there staring into space, arms akimbo, muttering over and again: "I understand . . . that is quite clear."

It seemed to me that Organtino was counting on this side of the Signore's character in his ambition to obtain a portion of the reclaimed land at the foot of the Azuchi hill, and I had no reason to doubt he would get what he wanted. Had not the Signore said, as they looked down from the window of the tower, that he might choose whatever spot he fancied?

"Yes," I said in support of Organtino's proposal, "I think there is every chance of obtaining the Signore's consent. If that location is the most advantageous, you should ask for it."

The land in question was located on a marshy plain that spread out into the lake from the foot of the hill, very close to the palace. If the town itself were compared to a fan, then this spot corresponded roughly to the pivot. As Organtino paced about the site, his expression revealed his satisfaction. The Azuchi Christians too agreed that the spot would be the best imaginable, though they doubted it would actually be granted them. This area of reclaimed land had been designated for the residences of vassals and retainers, and already a large number of houses had been constructed. Thus, unlike in the district set aside for commoners and merchants, there was little open land remaining.

When at last Organtino went to the palace with Lorenzo to make his request, the doubts of the Japanese Christians proved wholly unfounded, for the Signore appeared actually delighted that Organtino had found a spot that appealed to him.

"Well then, where is this place that pleases you so?" he said, jumping up without ceremony and going to the window of the tower.

"We are particularly drawn to the land that has been filled in by the lake, visible over there just above the top of that tree, near where the roads come together. A row of houses now stands on the spot, but there is vacant space among them." Leaning out of the window, Organtino pointed toward the spot where he wished to build his church.

"You speak of the land built up with houses girdled round with white walls?. . . So that is what pleases you. . . . Well, so it should! It is quite near, and I could pay you a visit from time to time." He laughed. "But do you not worry that it is too crowded there? A great number of houses have already gone up in that district, and the land still available might not be enough to build a church on a truly grand scale. In fact, I can tell already that it will be quite insufficient. So here is what we'll do: we will evict two of the neighboring households and the field beyond, and add that land to your site."

I had the impression at that moment that the Signore was already drawing imaginary buildings on the land, much as if he himself were designing the church. No doubt a basilica much like the one in Kyoto was already rising before his eyes. No doubt, too, he was recalling how Organtino had once told him that in Kyoto the church had not achieved its desired shape because of lack of space, and had ended up almost square. The church in Azuchi, I was sure, would be constructed in the rectangular form of a true basilica and on the most magnificent scale imaginable.

Organtino began to object that it would not do to disrupt others in order to build the church, but the Signore interrupted in the most serene of tones:

"No, please do not worry yourself on that account. I assure you that those affected will be most handsomely compensated. I shall look at the site tomorrow morning," he added to a retainer standing close at hand. "If construction is to commence immediately, the ground will have to be leveled."

The next morning, Organtino, Lorenzo, and I, along with a dozen of so of the Azuchi Christians, met the Signore at the appointed place. Dismounting, he looked around and said almost immediately:

"This seems indeed to be an excellent place to build a church." With characteristic dispatch, he started to pace restlessly about the site, giving instructions to his attendants.

"Fell that tree," he would say, or "Remove that stone," or "The man evicted from that house shall be paid. . . ," or "Have them removed to such and such a place."

When he had covered more or less the whole area, he glanced

back over the land and said to his advisers: "I am thinking I will give this place to the Christian fathers. What are your thoughts on the matter?"

"A church? Here?" said a handsome young attendant.

"Yes, just so. What do you think?" repeated the Signore.

The young man seemed about to say something, then, visibly mastering his original urge, managed to say:

"Doubtless a church would be a fitting ornament to the city. By all means let there be a church in Azuchi." He had sensed, as had I myself, that the Signore's remark was less a question than a decree.

The following day the Signore again went to view the land in the company of several of his closest advisers, this time without informing Organtino, and on this occasion he called together all the residents of the district. We were told later that his only instructions to them were to assist the Christians in every possible way in the construction of the church.

"When he speaks of the fathers," said the believer who recounted this meeting to us, "he refers to them almost as if they were his brothers. Over and again he said that they were to be respected, that they were good and brave men. Lord Takayama, too, was present among the Signore's company, and was called over to answer various questions about the building of a church. It is even said that the Signore was overheard remarking that the fathers alone seemed to have a reasonable explanation for everything in creation."

Recalling these words, I am astounded afresh at the trust and sincere friendship the Signore showed us, and am struck too by the frankness with which he expressed his feelings. I should add, my friend, that not a few at court maintained that his affections were politically motivated from start to finish, inspired as much by an undying hatred of the Buddhist bonzes as by anything else. Even the kindly Sakuma was among the cynical here. But it still seems to me that these people were simply incapable of understanding the Signore's true feelings. They were subtle, cunning men who doubtless felt sure they were divining the Signore's innermost heart, but in fact I feel they were twisting what was straightforward, warping what was true. I have already written of the Signore's isolation in his own court, and of the sinister motives with which his subjects seemed to have invested him. Perhaps the present difference in interpretations is just another example of this phenomenon. Yet for all my disagreement with these good courtiers as to the motives behind the Signore's friendship, I must admit that I did not, myself, have any simple explanation, and often found myself pondering its significance.

I was, however, not without some clues to the puzzle. There was the smile on the Signore's face, so full of loneliness and regret, each time we took our leave. Then there was the time when, on my way home from the parade grounds, I chanced to glimpse the Signore walking along a passage connecting two pavilions of his palace. His expression, so extremely dark and desolate, had shocked me deeply. It was not an expression he wore in our presence. He might, I felt, have worn it in the midst of bloody battle—yet there was something there still sterner, still sadder, something I have no words to describe, except to say that it was almost as though suffering had carved a deep, indelible mark on his brow.

Some part of the gloom, of course, derived from the political difficulties involved in the subjugation of Ishiyama and from the continued jousting with the forces of Mori. But the look on the Signore's face was not due merely to external circumstances. It came from within, from the Signore's very way of life. It was a look that came naturally to the face of a man who was forever testing his limits, who was ceaselessly driving himself on....

However—I was telling you of the special nature of our friendship with the Signore, a friendship that deepened still further in later times when the building in Azuchi was complete and he came to visit us. If it was I he talked with, we would discuss navigation, say, or astronomy, or any one of the other natural sciences. At such times something in his manner of questioning always seemed to betray a great thirst for knowledge. I had felt it when, years before in Gifu, he asked about the arquebus and methods of fortification. It may be that his interest in knowledge as such was all the greater in that there was no pressing need now to put it to use in a current war. Perhaps he was particularly struck by the power of knowledge that could build a better gun, or great ships capable of taking men to the ends of the earth. This may be why he always made a wry face at the sight of believers or bonzes of the Buddhist faith, as if they were unclean beasts.

"Their 'knowledge,'" he would say at such times, "is nothing but empty, useless phrases. What I need is knowledge that is true and thus able to change the face of the world—a knowledge that can bring things to pass."

Perhaps the Signore's lack of patience with what he felt to be a useless existence wasted in fruitless debates stemmed from the sense of purpose informing everything in his own life. From the time he rose early in the morning to the time he retired, his life was filled with warfare and politics. Matters requiring his attention confronted him one after the other: strategic conferences, reports from the front lines, plans to increase the production of guns, the handling of the transport of provisions, the reorganization of the lands of Gokinai, preparations for the assessment and collection of taxes, the maintenance of the public peace in the cities of his domain, the need to keep a say in the workings of village governments, the building of roads, bridges, and dams, the reform of the system of highways and inns. Among these problems were some that had reached a critical juncture and demanded a quick decision, others that required more basic, long-term planning. There were some decisions on which he would

148

consult his advisers at length, others that he made alone. In every instance, though, he viewed the problem according to his principle that all things should develop to completion along rational lines. Thus the way that Akechi came to rank with Hashiba as one of his favorite ministers, though due in part to the former's coolly calculated strategies and skill in attacking fortresses, was also rumored to derive in part from his administrative ability in handling lands and tax systems.

As the man responsible for handling such practical problems, the Signore was in constant need of ways and means to urge things along to their logical and natural conclusion—the thing he called *koto ga naru* in his own tongue—and it was this that led him to thirst so avidly after knowledge. But as I said before, the knowledge that interested him was not the pedantic learning of the scribes but the precious, hard-won knowledge of practical experience and rational inquiry.

"Approach your duties with the same courage and steadfastness the Christian fathers showed in setting out to cross the seas." Such was the Signore's admonition to his retainers on more than one occasion. In fact, even he seemed at times to find it difficult to understand why anyone would make such a voyage. He had been known to ask Organtino quite directly why he had come to Japan, and would speculate, with a laugh, that the fathers perhaps had not come to evangelize at all, but for some more secret and sinister purpose. Nevertheless, whatever he thought the real reason to be, he admired and sympathized with the fierce determination and energy that had brought them such a distance to live in such precarious circumstances.

The sympathy was due to the fact that he too, like the fathers, was willing to give up whatever he had—his ideas, his feelings, his habits, his beliefs, his honor, even his self-respect—for the sake of his *koto ga naru*. And the notorious harshness of his reign derived from the simple fact that he demanded the same sort of attitude from generals, vassals, and *daimyos* alike. He demanded, in short, absolute commitment, not to his person, but to the principle to which he was devoted, to *koto ga naru*. For this most concrete of abstractions, they were expected to sacrifice their own desires, overcome their sense of self, and walk with their leader the narrow path of reason. I realized that the mark of suffering I had seen carved on the Signore's brow was due only in part to continual self-discipline and self-denial; it was deepened by a loneliness born of the awe and sense of remoteness that his merciless demands inspired in those about him.

But for all the suffering and loneliness I had seen on the Signore's face in one of his unguarded moments, Organtino and I knew another, very different man—the one who was now throwing himself into the construction of a church in Azuchi. For it was no lonely and somber being who planned to surprise Organtino by personally going to inspect the site. What sort of being then, *was* he? Even allowing for every possible friendly feeling the Signore may have cherished toward any or all of us (or, to put it more cynically, for every conceivable political motive), it still seemed extraordinary that the sovereign prince of a great kingdom should wander abroad to investigate a plot of land for a heathen church. I could picture him, nonetheless, in just that improbable activity: kicking away small stones, or having his retainers remove debris cluttering the ground, busily imagining the form and disposition of the buildings that would one day occupy the site. I could see his face as he stood watching the retainers clear the land, its expression the same as on the day when the news of Araki's rebellion was brought to Azuchi and he stared out at the waves on the lake.

You will think me frivolous, I fear, for speculating at such length about the state of mind of a man I knew so long ago and in such a distant kingdom, but you must humor me, remembering that I have had a great deal of time to recall these things as I sit in my chamber here in Goa. Indeed, I have had little heart for much else. . . .

Be that as it may, as the Signore watched the preparations for the church, he seemed to grow melancholy. I suspect it was from a longing to discuss his new project, the church, with one of his own. At that moment, the two men with whom he might have hoped to share his excitement were both away at the front implementing his strategy against the Mori. I do not, frankly, know just what he might have hoped for from them. Hashiba, no doubt, would have found the whole notion of a church in Azuchi slightly ludicrous and made something of a joke, albeit a polite one, of the Signore's enthusiasm—though in the end he would have said that if a church were to be built, at any rate it should at least be magnificent. Perhaps the Signore craved Hashiba's lively cheerfulness precisely because it was so often mixed with a sharp, almost vitriolic wit.

The other man at the front, Akechi, would have offered the Signore a very different kind of companionship. He would never have laughed off this or any other matter, and though his manner was perhaps rather dull compared to Hashiba's, he would no doubt have understood the Signore's friendship for Organtino, and have divined the real significance of the Azuchi church.

Such speculations aside, it was clear to everyone that the good will displayed by the Signore was something out of the ordinary, though few among the vassals or even the Christians seemed capable of understanding its nature. Organtino himself admitted that he had not expected such enthusiasm from the Signore—enthusiasm such as almost to suggest that the Signore himself had commissioned the construction.

Now Organtino, in planning this new project, took into account the fact that the Visitor-General to the mission, Valignano, had arrived in Kyushu the previous year. He knew that once Valignano had made his rounds in the south, he would come to

Kyoto as well, and was thus inclined to postpone construction until after Valignano's visit. This idea, however, did not sit at all well with the Japanese Christians; in particular the men of substance and position among them were steadfastly opposed to delaying the work. They held that it was absolutely vital to respond to such an unusual show of benevolence on the part of the Signore, and that some sort of building must be erected immediately: "If the fortunes of our faith have indeed risen to the point where the Signore himself is commanding the construction of a church in Azuchi, then we may perhaps hope for an end once and for all to the prejudice and persecutions that have dogged us thus far. But we feel strongly that it would increase the dignity and credibility of the church if we could begin construction immediately."

Lord Takayama was of the same mind and offered to assume responsibility for various aspects of the construction just as he had done in Kyoto:

"I will do whatever I can. Let us lose no time in gathering the necessary timber, plaster, and stones, and I will see to procuring the men to move and assemble them. We must act at once. We must show ourselves willing and able to respond to the Signore's support; if we do so, I have no doubt it will work in favor of the church at large. By the same token, should we hesitate over plans and the like, failing to make a prompt start even though we have received permission to build, it will reflect unfavorably—particularly on those of us who hold rank in the Signore's court. You have heard, I believe, that the Signore has been seen on more than one occasion making personal inspections of the site. I intend no disrespect, but it seems to me that he is waiting for the church much as a child waits impatiently for a new toy. He must not be disappointed."

I too felt it advisable to begin the work immediately, but my reasons were not the political concerns of the Christians. I merely feared that if construction were delayed the Signore might slip back into the dark despair I sensed was haunting him.

It happened that around that time the materials necessary for construction of a missionary hall and seminary to be erected in affiliation with the church in Kyoto had been assembled in that city. The greater part of the timber, it seemed, had already been cut and fitted by the carpenters, and was simply awaiting a frame. Recalling this, I suggested to Organtino that we bring this lumber to Azuchi. I was aware that the church in Kyoto had already outgrown its building, but the capital at least had a church of a kind, whereas here in Azuchi there was nothing at all. Moreover, while the construction of a mission hall and a seminary in the capital might make things considerably more convenient and comfortable for the fathers, it was unlikely to provide any immediate benefit for the body of believers, or to prove particularly useful in impressing the Buddhist bonzes. Thus—I argued to Organtino—to bring the lumber to Azuchi and construct the planned buildings on the land granted us by the Signore would not only allow us to begin construction almost immediately, but would also be the most effective husbanding of resources.

In fact, it seems, the same thought had already occurred to the father himself. He pointed out that before proceeding with this plan it would be necessary to obtain the permission of the newly arrived Visitor-General, Father Valignano, as well as the consent of the congregation in Kyoto. Nevertheless, in outline, we had struck on a scheme that met with the approval of all.

"A splendid solution indeed," said Lord Takayama. "Some may say that we ignore spiritual priorities in building a mission hall and *seminario* before we even have a church, but the truly pressing need is for some—any—Christian edifice here in Azuchi. I, for one, am delighted at the thought of a *seminario*, and will send as many young men as possible from my domain to study here. It is an exciting prospect." Judging from the nods and exclamations of agreement during this short speech, Takayama's ideas were shared generally. And this good Christian lord soon backed his words with deeds, sending fifteen hundred coolies to Kyoto to transport the building materials. Other grandees sympathetic to the cause followed suit, while believers of humbler rank as well, just as during the building of the church in Kyoto, gathered together to help with the new project.

The Visitor-General sent his approval directly. Even before it reached us, the work of bringing the materials to Azuchi was under way. Then, once it was obtained, several thousands more were added to the company of men pushing carts and urging oxen on toward the new castle. The sight of this enormous procession bearing wood and stone came as something of a shock to the citizens of Kyoto: it was during the campaign against Ishiyama that they had last seen such large numbers of men on the move. This time, however, it was the banner of the cross rather than battle ensigns that flew over the great line as, like an army of ants, it wound its way east along the highway to Azuchi, where all was now in readiness.

When this procession had finally made its way to the Signore's new capital and the materials were gathered together, we immediately raised a frame and began to assemble the building just as it had been planned for the site in Kyoto. This work differed from the construction of the Church of the Ascension in the sense that we now had ample land on which to build and we lacked nothing in the way of materials, neither lumber nor stones. As a result, the mission hall we constructed was even grander and more spacious than the greatest mansion of the lords and generals who lived in the surrounding streets.

As the building took shape, the Signore made frequent appearances, mounted on his horse, at the construction site. Each time, he was obliged to order the workers back to their tasks, since they invariably stopped and stared in awe at the sight of such an august visitor. Riding about the area, he would listen to reports from the head carpenter or whatever other supervisor happened to be present. Occasionally, Organtino or I would explain some feature of the building, and the Signore would question us at length about various aspects of Italian architecture. The mission hall we were building had three floors with walls rising perpendicular on all four sides, so that apart from the porch and the belfry it was a more or less perfect cube. Concerning this simplicity of form, the Signore commented that in the buildings of his kingdom it was the custom to make the second story smaller than the first and the third smaller again than the second, each story being decorated with its own roof. "Do you not agree," he added, "that such a design is a good deal more stable, as well as more pleasing?"

"I will confess," Organtino answered, "that I have often marveled at the complexity and refinement of your buildings, and at their delicacy. There is, for example, nothing in all the palaces and cathedrals of Europe to compare with the joining of the roofs, in which you so excel. The aim of our architecture, however, is different. We seek to reduce all forms to the simplest relationship between horizontal and vertical.

"There are, of course, other differences which must not be forgotten. In Europe, for example, the principal material of most structures is stone, a fact that cannot help but influence the form. There are two aspects of our structure that are worth pointing out. One is the way in which walls rising straight to the roof afford the greatest possible interior space—in this building alone, we will have thirty-four separate chambers equipped with balconies. The other is the solidity of the building—fully two hundred people might live here at once, yet you would never hear so much as the sound of a creaking pillar.

"Even leaving aside the question of strength, I think you will agree that a building in your style—with its successively smaller stories—would yield barely half the number of rooms for the same amount of materials."

The Signore listened to Organtino's speech with profound attention. I never afterward heard that he said anything to criticize Organtino's argument, and it was indeed common enough for him to simply listen in thoughtful silence. Not that he abstained from his usual questions: indeed, he inquired eagerly about various features of the building, probing further and deeper whenever something in the answer escaped him. The questions were similar to those that the globe had provoked, but with an added eagerness and delight, as if the mission hall were his own special project.

One day, he stopped at the construction site on the way home from falconing, still dressed in the deerskin trousers called *hakama* which he wore to the hunt. Calling aside one of the foremen, he asked what kind of tile was to be used on the roof of the building.

"The same black tile that was used on the church in Kyoto," said the foreman, bowing his head. "There was neither the time nor the money to have special tiles fired for the building."

"Did you make this decision yourself?" asked the Signore.

"No, my lord. Organtino-sama and the others were all agreed on the matter."

"Well, then, they must change their minds. We will use the blue tiles from the *castello* instead. You may place an order at your convenience for the required number and types. Yes—" he continued, as if to himself, "harmonizing this building with the castle will, I am sure, produce a most pleasing effect."

The Signore's order was immediately relayed to Organtino, who had temporarily returned to Kyoto. He was unsure how to interpret this fresh show of beneficence from the Signore, and paced about the room, much as Father Frois had done in his time, as he pondered the new development—for it could hardly have been called a problem. The ability to read the secret thoughts of others was not, I fear, among the gifts of this simple peasant from Brescia; but his puzzlement at least was understandable, since no one would claim that it was easy to read the mind of the Signore. One thing that was clear was that this latest show of generosity went beyond the bounds of simple goodwill. Despite the ostensible motive—the desire to reconcile the color of the tiles with that of the *palazzo*—the gift of tiles made exclusively for the fortress amounted to a show of very special patronage. No doubt Sakuma and the others would have read self-interest into even this gesture; but Organtino was of a different mind. Himself a virtuous man, he tended to assume virtue in others, and to him a show of good will was that and no more. As he paced the room, his friendly eyes were shining. "No," he said, "I think we should accept his offer thankfully. With Father Frois's permission we must find gifts from amongst our store of European goods that will convey our appreciation to the Signore."

As if concurring with Organtino's view, the workers at the construction site seemed to labor all the more feverishly in the days that followed, hurrying to complete the building quickly in accordance with the Signore's wishes. Even before dawn, the Christian men would come to the construction site to begin planing wood and spreading plaster by the light of bonfires. By the time the sun came up, the whole area would be so crowded that there was barely room for everyone to work, and the sound of the foremen's voices mingled with the striking of hammers. The mixture of skilled workers and untrained but exceedingly enthusiastic Christians made for considerable confusion, yet a tenuous kind of order, a hair's-breadth from chaos, was always maintained at the site.

I myself was away on a brief excursion to the north of the lake at this time, and learned of the matter of the blue tiles on my return. I, of course, had absolutely no quarrel with the general appreciation of the Signore's patronage expressed by the Christians, nor with the desire of Organtino and the rest to respond in kind. Nevertheless, my reaction was somewhat different from those around me. The Signore's gesture, it struck me at once, was less a show of friendship than the sad, almost desperate beckoning of a lonely man; less a matter of aesthetics than of the suffering that had invaded the deepest recesses of the Signore's heart. I was reminded of the sentimental gestures of soldiers who exchange crosses or other mementoes as symbols of friendship on the eve of a battle that promises to be particularly bloody.

I myself have had an experience that is relevant here; you will forgive me, my friend, if I relate it, for I think it may shed some light on the Signore's frame of mind in offering us his blue tiles.

It was in the jungles of Nuova Spagna that I once gave a gold chain—a keepsake from my mother—to a young sergeant who served as my aide-de-camp all through that ill-fated campaign. A purely sentimental gesture, you may say—yet I am still sure, all these years later, that it was nothing of the kind. My gift was in no sense intended to curry favor with the young man, nor even as a sign of appreciation for his faithful service. Even so, my real feelings are difficult to put into words. I remember how deeply that lonely figure struck me—a young man, grown old in the space of a fortnight, covered with mud and bowed with weariness yet continuing to perform his duties despite everything. It conveyed nothing at all heroic or spectacular; it represented a simple will to survive at best—at worst, a futile effort in an ill-conceived cause that held no prospect of success. Yet still the man continued to do his best, irrespective of the outcome, with never the least complaint, much as if the whole point of his brief life lay in the correct execution of my orders. Shouldering his heavy share of the ammunition, he slashed his way through the jungle, all the while doing what he could to encourage the soldiers in our charge. When night fell, he slept as if dead; I remember seeing his old-young face in the weak light of the moon and feeling a strange familiarity, a sense of closeness.

I myself at the time had begun to question the reasonableness of our commander's orders. I, too, was acting solely from a sense of obligation to complete a task once undertaken. The thought that I was leading others in a campaign that I knew to be futile troubled me, and it was all I could do to live with the knowledge. But then it occurred to me that the young man was bearing a similar burden—bore it, moreover, with no outward sign of resentment. The realization was what increased my feeling of kinship with him. It was not that I pitied him, nor even, precisely, that I sympathized with him. Nor do I believe that I myself was looking for sympathy or consolation. We were simply two men, each of us walking a similar lonely path.

When I heard of the matter of the blue tiles, it was this young man who immediately came to mind. I realize, of course, the difference between my situation as leader of a small band of men on a hopeless mission and the Signore's as ruler of a vast realm; yet I sensed a loneliness behind this architectural gesture that reminded me somehow of my own feelings about the gold chain all those years ago in the jungle. . . .

Not a month had elapsed before construction of the mission hall was complete. The windows on each floor had Venetian blinds. The three-story central structure had a belfry that rose higher than the rest, and a cloister running round an inner courtyard. Gray paint, brought by one of the Portuguese trading ships, had been used on the outer walls, and the window frames were edged in white in the Venetian manner. The blinds and doors were green, and above everything the blue tiles, the mark of the Signore's beneficence, glistened as if in salute to the castle on the hill.

I was unable to attend the celebration of the mission's completion, having been summoned to Kyushu by some of the generals with whom I had worked in Lord Kuki's navy. However, a letter from Organtino informed me that more than twenty thousand of the faithful gathered for the ceremony, among them many who had come from Kyoto and the Gokinai provinces. Those who came from afar were particularly moved, they said, by their first glimpse of the mission building from the Azuchi highway, rising shining above all the other buildings around it.

"It seems," Organtino wrote, "that the blessings to be reaped from this building will be even greater than we had hoped. Its close proximity to the castle, combined with the gift of the blue tiles, has given currency to rumors that the Signore has all but embraced our faith. Some quarters are whispering that it is not the Signore but his sons who have converted to the church—and, I have, in fact, received a request from those young men to build a church and a mission in Gifu as soon as possible. We are going to be busy with our architectural duties, it seems, since the Signore too, in his speech at the dedication, urged that we build the church here in Azuchi in the very near future.

"As things are going, nobody who is already a Christian or thinking of becoming one is going to be able to leave Azuchi for long to come. It is particularly gratifying to see heathen generals and *daimyo*s among those who gather to hear the sermons. So many are being baptized every day that I have felt compelled to write to Visitor-General Valignano requesting that he send as many padres as can be spared to assist with the work here in Azuchi."

Both the church in Kyoto and the mission in Azuchi were regularly so crowded by now that people overflowed into the streets, whence they peered in at the windows, straining to hear the words of the sermons and the hymns. If one recalled the condition of the church in this kingdom only a few years since— when Father Vilela huddled in that decaying house, shivering as the wind blew through holes in the paper doors, delivering homilies to a handful of men and women—its recent successes seemed all but incredible. Nor was it only the church that had changed—it would hardly be an exaggeration to say that a new age had dawned in the kingdom of Japan. In those days, the capital had been a chaotic battlefield where fearsome mounted warriors filled the streets and the sound of fighting was heard day and night. The smoke of burning towns and villages hung in the sky. Father Vilela and Father Frois had no grand church then to protect them, and the bonzes and citizens of the capital had pelted them with stones and driven them from the city.

But Kyoto by the time the new mission was completed in Azuchi was a different place altogether. Relief and happiness could be sensed in every quarter of the city. Ruined houses had been repaired, new ones were under construction, and the lively sound of hammering filled the air. Under the Signore's tutelage, a police force had been installed, and the watch in each street had been strengthened so that the work of burglars, vandals, and other mischief makers had become unprofitable. Merchants had returned to the boulevards in great numbers, and little theaters and tent shows were again attracting an audience. The women of the pleasure quarters came back from the provinces and could be seen in their bright *quimonos*, beckoning to customers. The very streets had become a stage where people played on instruments, monkey trainers beat their drums, and dancing women displayed their talents.

The mood in Azuchi was nearly as lively. The mansions of the gentry, with gleaming white walls, now filled the strip of land between the castle and the lake. Elsewhere, the woods had been cut and thickets thinned, and new shops and other buildings were beginning to line the streets. Soldiers and travelers were on the move on the highway, and the inns were constantly full. Many of the newcomers were merchants attracted by stories of the prosperity of the new city. Moreover, settlers in Azuchi had been exempted of certain taxes and corvée labor, and other incentives had been devised to swell the population of the town.

The forces of Lord Mori continued to offer resistance in the west, but the fighting there seemed distant to people who had lived so long in the midst of war. At last, the citizens of Kyoto and the surrounding provinces were enjoying a spell of peace, as if a long, dreary winter had finally passed and left in its wake the flowers of spring.

The change was most palpable the following year when I first attended the outdoor feast that the Japanese call *hanami*, or "the viewing of flowers." Traveling to the outskirts of Kyoto for the occasion, I was greeted by a most extraordinary sight: a large area of ground beneath a great cloud of white and pink blossoms floating above gnarled black trees had been cordoned off with curtains and hangings. Couches were placed here and there, and the ground was spread with scarlet carpets. In this lovely "room" with its living ceiling, the guests were drinking saké and sampling delicacies from exquisitely made boxes. Some were clapping time with their hands while others sang and danced wildly, stomping about with arms around each other's shoulders. There was a great deal of shouting and laughter, all to the accompaniment of various musical instruments. I was quite struck by this sudden show of high spirits from people who were generally rather reserved. In part, it occurred to me, it must be the pent-up energy of men and women who had lived for a long while under a cloud of anxiety and fear; the cloud had at last lifted, and they had come out together to dance in the open air.

The cherry blossom—for it was a variety of cherry that formed our delightful bower—bloomed riotously, every black twig crowded with clusters of delicate white petals slightly tinged with crimson, and the revelers below were riotous in due proportion. I was continually being pressed to drink by one or another of the drunken guests, in the importunate manner that Organtino and Frois found so difficult to understand. To me, it was a splendid sight, in a sense, to see these people, normally so reasonable and moderate, gradually succumbing to intoxication. Nor did I have any inclination to upbraid their "weakness"; sometimes it is weakness that makes people lovable.

In the evening, as we were preparing to return to the city, the wind came up, creating a sight to marvel at: a sudden blizzard of petals flying up and swirling down on the mad dancers below.

We were told later that a similar *hanami* feast had been held at Azuchi. Throughout the kingdom there was a feeling that this was a celebration, not just of the blossoms of spring but of the flowering of the Signore's reign.

It was in March of fifteen eighty-one, just as the flowers were reaching their full splendor in the hills, that the Visitor-General to the mission, an impressive and fine-looking man named Alessandro Valignano, left Kyushu and appeared in the Gokinai region. Even before leaving Goa to assume his post as Visitor to the Parish of Japan, he had been something of a legend for his fierce ambition, his piercing intelligence, and most of all for his allegedly debauched past. Again and again—though always furtively—the story was told of his days at the university in Padua, when he had been in the habit of visiting taverns in the company of questionable women, spending days on end in a state of drunkenness, involving himself in violent arguments that often ended in bloodshed. The friars seemed to be particularly well informed and enthusiastic about these tales of the Visitor's "descent into Hell," and whispered them endlessly amongst themselves.

I also heard them tell a still sadder story of his rage at his lover's perfidy, a rage that had led him to cut her face to shreds. It was said that while atoning for that crime in the jail of Venice, he had received God's grace, and upon his release had finally learned the meaning of love in the forgiveness of the woman he had scarred. Hearing the story, I could not help recalling the evil day when I stabbed my wife in Genoa. In our different ways, Valignano and I had both plunged into that perilous ravine separating love and hate, and had seen our whole lives consumed in its fires.

I was also conscious, however, of a difference between our lives since then. I myself, as you know, have occupied every waking hour with this battle with destiny, have staked everything on the affirmation of my own life and will. Valignano, I was given to understand—and later saw for myself—did just the opposite. Preoccupied with self-denial, he had spent his whole life seeking to overcome his past through penance and abnegation. His mistress's face had been the fairest in all Verona, but he remembered it only as it had appeared on the day she had come to visit him, wrapped in a dark veil to hide the scars; the memory, I was certain, came still to haunt his dreams, and I knew from my own experience the indescribable despair he would feel at finding the murky passions of his younger days alive, unchanged, within him. He knew, as I did, that he was exactly the same person that had done that evil deed: the certainty gnawed at him as he lay down at night and when he arose at dawn. How many days were tainted with this thought, how many sleepless nights were spent attending to the business of the church, in simple penances, in endless reading from the holy fathers, all in the hope of forgetfulness?

I was convinced that Valignano's decision to leave the land of his birth and become Visitor-General to the diocese of India was related to this desire to atone, to carve in his own being the marks he had once inflicted on another. He had been born to a noble family of Padua, but never once made mention of his aristocratic origins. His reticence on this point made for a strange contrast with his predecessor as the ranking member of the mission, for Father Cabral had missed no opportunity to offer arrogant reminders that he was the highborn son of a Portuguese grandee.

Stories of the antagonism between the two men had circulated for two years, since the time of Father Valignano's arrival in

Japan. At a conference in Kuchinotsu, it was said, a dispute of some violence had erupted, Valignano placing himself squarely in opposition to the policies of Father Cabral. No doubt there was a basic conflict of character. I would imagine, for instance, that the Visitor-General had disapproved of the extreme contempt and disdain the Vice-Provincial showed toward the Japanese—his personal prejudice, in effect, against his entire congregation. In short, the intolerance of Cabral's attitude as a whole might well have seemed (as it had to me) counterproductive to the work of the mission.

Such criticisms of Cabral were not entirely new. Even the gentle Organtino had been known to voice them from time to time, and I myself had launched vociferous, if sporadic, diatribes against the man ever since we had shared the same ship on the voyage from the Malaccas. In all probability, Organtino's views had been communicated to the Visitor-General while he was still in Goa, so that by the time of the latter's meeting with Cabral in Kuchinotsu and his inspection of the churches in Kyushu, his opinions were already formed.

Perhaps it would be best to see the dealings between Valignano and Cabral simply as a disagreement over how best to run a mission. Yet I could not help picturing to myself the scene at the meeting, knowing as I did that Cabral would hardly have resisted the temptation to take advantage of his opponent's infamous past. No doubt, he had flaunted his supposed superiority with all the narrow-minded arrogance a Portuguese noble could muster. In any case, there could have been little common ground between the two men. One of them was almost blinded by his burning self-absorption and self-confidence, the other forever seeking to get beyond himself, to surpass himself—on the one side intolerance and bombast, on the other, cool melancholy, resignation, and hard-won serenity.

I should tell you now, though it may be plain enough already, that even before I met Valignano I sensed some bond between us, had lively intimations that he, too, had come to this distant land in search of something.

I first met him when he arrived in Kyoto some ten days after his ship reached Sakai. A great crowd of the faithful came along with his party, surrounding it as if it were a festival procession. Before coming to Kyoto, he had presided at a solemn celebration of Easter Mass in the church at Lord Takayama's castle, and it seemed that people had not yet recovered from the excitement and emotion of that occasion. One of the Christians described the scene for me. Upward of fifteen thousand believers had crowded in and around the church. Noble warriors and their wives in all their finery, together with the young seminarians in white robes, had gone in procession to the church waving the palm fronds of victory and bearing aloft the sacred pictures. Many of the people were carrying torches and lanterns to light the way. Finally, beneath a canopy carried by acolytes, came Valignano himself, holding the sacred relics. Organtino and Frois followed in their festival raiments of shining gold brocade. Great crowds lined the road all the way, scattering flowers in the procession's path and cheering when they caught sight of the principal; it was plain to all present that this was the most splendid celebration the church had yet observed in this kingdom.

Following the Mass, a great banquet was held, but most of those in attendance continued to pray and sing hymns; some, even, were so overcome with joy that they could do nothing but weep quietly. "Ever since Valignano-sama arrived in Sakai," said the man who described these events for me, "I have followed him everywhere, and the number of believers and curiosity seekers who gather around him has increased daily. I wonder where his fame will stop? The crowds overflow into the street, and when he walks by the river, people follow in boats just to catch a glimpse of him. He has only to appear to throw an entire town into an uproar."

I myself had caught only a glimpse of him, on horseback, over the heads of the crowd as he made his way to the church in Kyoto. The people were held back by a line of guards sent by the governor, our friend Lord Murai, but the restraint only fanned their excitement. Screams could be heard here and there, and quarrels broke out among those straining for a better view.

Not all this ardent curiosity was generated by the tall and handsome Valignano alone; in part, it was due to the servant who accompanied him to carry the canopy, a black man named Geronimo. There was a great surge of people toward the procession as he passed; at the height of the pushing and shoving, someone fell in a ditch and broke his leg, while another was driven up against a wall with enough force to make him lose consciousness. The fences and gates of several houses along the way were completely demolished, according to my informant. In the end, it was the news of Geronimo's arrival that swept most rapidly and widely through the city. His reputation was instantaneous and complete, inspiring such crowds that I gave up trying to meet Valignano there in the street and returned to the church ahead of their parade—only to find it, too, surrounded by a great crowd awaiting the arrival of the black man.

Geronimo, I learned in the days that followed, had spent his youth in our native Genoa. He had the cheery nature of his race. Before becoming associated with Valignano, he had been a porter on the docks—one of my own former occupations, you will remember—then a waiter, and finally a mercenary, in which capacity he had roamed the world. His acquaintance with the Visitor-General dated from a chance encounter in which Valignano had rescued him from some ruffians who were beating him for failure to pay a small debt. . . .

Such was the man who had thus achieved instant fame in the kingdom of Japan—a fame, indeed, that had already reached the ears of the Signore himself. Happening at the time to be in residence at the *palazzo* in Kyoto, he sent word that very day that he would like to meet the black man.

Arrived at the church, the followers promptly started complaining at Geronimo for causing the crush: one man had had his clothing ripped; another had suffered an injury to his leg; a third had lost his hat. Geronimo did not seem particularly perturbed by the uproar he was causing, and in fact seemed to be rather enjoying himself. When the Signore's messenger arrived, he did not even wait for a cue from Organtino, but immediately responded that he would be pleased to go to the *palazzo*.

I myself was not present at this audience with the Signore, but Organtino later reported the details to me with his customary thoroughness. The palace, normally rather subdued when the Signore was present, was extremely lively that day, and the attendants hurried to line the corridors as Geronimo approached. Whispers ran down the halls like wind rippling through wheat: "They have dyed him with India ink." "Do you suppose he is black all over?" Or simply, "How could any man ever be so black?"

The Signore himself seemed truly startled at the sight of Geronimo, and refused at first to believe that the color of his skin was, in fact, natural. However, when told that the deep hue was thought to be the result of generation upon generation being burned by the sun, he at last seemed to understand. As was his wont, he had the globe brought in and listened intently to a description of this land where the sun shone so fiercely, the land where black people lived. Finally, he bade Geronimo remove his shirt, and when he had inspected him a while longer, at last seemed satisfied with what he had seen and heard.

Afterward, they set out to visit the Signore's son at his *palazzo*.

People gathered around him, rubbing his skin, taking off his clothing, and finally, even, carrying him off to one of their baths where they scrubbed him to try to remove the color.

When they arrived at the residence of the Signore's son, Geronimo, who was not without a certain theatrical sense, decided to attempt one of the Japanese greetings Organtino had taught him. He brought it off quite well, much to the astonishment and admiration of the young lord, and they were told that Geronimo was to return to the *palazzo* each day. There was a story that as they were about to take leave of the prince, Geronimo had demonstrated his considerable bodily strength by lifting two enormous stone mortars, one on each arm, and bursting out of a stout rope that he had bound around his body.

Valignano himself had not been present at these meetings, and it seemed clear to me that Organtino was skillfully paving the way to assure that the Visitor made a good impression on the Signore at their first meeting. Otherwise, it would have made little sense to send the servant—even such a famous black one—in advance of the master. In any case, the first interview between the Signore and Valignano took place on the morning of the second day following the presentation of Geronimo. In addition to the Visitor-General himself, the party that proceeded to the palace consisted of Organtino, Father Frois, Lorenzo, three or four of the other padres, and myself. The gifts that Organtino had selected for the occasion drew up the rear, loaded in a palanquin: golden candlesticks from Lisbon, woolens from Florence, a carpet woven with the figure of a lion, glass from Venice, and an armchair covered in red velvet with decorations of gold. . . .

This audience was very different from my first meeting with the Signore in Gifu in the company of Vice-Provincial Cabral. The Signore's modest dress and his alert bearing were as ever, but everything else was quite changed. To begin with, there was the difference between Gifu and Kyoto—between a rural fortress and a great capital. Yet more than just the place, the very times themselves had changed. The court in this new age dressed in splendor and extravagance, and everything in the furnishings and decoration bespoke a new luxury.

Our own mood on this occasion was also, I need hardly say, most unlike the anxiety we had felt in Cabral's company. Now we were quite at ease—were rather proud, in fact, to be escorting a man such as Valignano. Of majestic—one might almost have said heroic—appearance, he stood a full head above the rest of us, and his skin was deeply tanned from the sun of Goa and Malacca. His features were strong and aristocratic, his manner cool and contemplative. Although he hardly had the easy sociability, cheerfulness, and liveliness of Organtino, he had a gift for careful observation and meticulous reasoning, as well as for grasping accurately the state of missionary work and forming bold and far-reaching plans. He was particularly determined to overturn Cabral's interdictions, especially those against establishing church schools and seminaries throughout the kingdom, against catechizing the natives, and against the supporting of church finances with income from the Portuguese trade. As far as he was able, Valignano made it his business to correct the prejudices of his predecessor, even in such matters as trusting the finances of local churches to the Japanese friars, and—if I may be allowed a more personal note—granting me the privilege of teaching science and mathematics at the *seminario* in Azuchi.

Unlike Organtino, Valignano was not overawed by the Signore—nor, in fact, was he even particularly impressed by him at first. Yet neither did he show Cabral's need to insist on his own dignity, or his haughtiness and pride. It may be that a long habit of enduring inner suffering had simply taught him to remain calm and aloof. His manner indeed, though respectful, was somewhat distant.

The Signore, however, was clearly fascinated by the Visitor

almost from the first glance. No doubt this was due in part to Valignano's cool, resolute manner; more important, though, was the fact, which quickly became apparent, that this newcomer was superior in learning to any of the priests who had preceded him in the lands east of India. Even his reputation for fierce ambition was due, perhaps, to the abundance and depth of his knowledge and his tireless mental activity. When, for example, the globe was produced during the first meeting in response to questions about Valignano's voyage, the Signore was treated to talk of lands, customs, and a host of other things such as he had never heard of before.

Hearing that Valignano's birthplace of Padua was only a few hundred leagues from the towns which Organtino and I called home, he asked the Visitor to speak to him of this land called Italia. Valignano employed a great many similes and comparisons in describing such things as the prosperity of Rome, the magnificence of the Basilica of Saint Peter at the Vatican and of the High Masses held there, commerce in Venice, the system of government in Florence, together with its arts and industries, and the culture and topography of Europe as a whole. The Signore showed special interest at the mention of the great edifice called Saint Peter's; would the said building, he inquired, be twice the size of the church in Kyoto?

"Oh dear, no," said, Valignano, shaking his head. "The church here is quite small compared to the Basilica of Saint Peter."

"Perhaps, my lord," interrupted Organtino, "it would be simplest to imagine the great keep of the castle at Azuchi built entirely of stone. . . ."

"But is such a building possible?" asked the Signore, clearly quite skeptical.

On a piece of paper, Organtino sketched a domed roof and vaults, explaining the method of laying the stones and how the ceiling was constructed.

"Well—that seems reasonable enough," the Signore replied eventually, "but as for the claim that this building is greater than the castle at Azuchi—one would find that difficult to believe without seeing it with one's own eyes." And he folded his arms and stared at the drawing as Lorenzo translated his words for Valignano.

"Without seeing it with one's own eyes . . . ," Valignano echoed to himself, and he too stared at the drawing as if thinking about something else altogether.

This initial meeting lasted about three hours. The Signore was animated throughout, and did nothing to modify the usual warm tone of his relations with Organtino and myself. When the time came for us to leave, he presented Valignano with ten ducks which had just been brought from the eastern provinces. The Visitor-General failed perhaps to grasp the full significance of such a gift but, as Organtino explained, it was an exceptional expression of favor. Within a few hours, word of it had spread throughout Kyoto. Rumor had it that the ducks had been hung on the front of the church, and a great many people actually came to see them—to their disappointment, of course.

You will perhaps appreciate, my friend, the change in mood that had come over this country, now that I have described some of its manifestations: the great and boisterous crowds that besieged Geronimo, the sumptuous banquets on the flowering hills, the throngs celebrating Easter at the church of Lord Takayama. In such ways, the people were expressing their joy at the return of peaceful days. For the Christians, the arrival of Valignano was particularly exciting, coinciding as it did with the advent of Easter, and the Church of the Ascension was full every day. At the hours of Mass, the entrances were choked with people, and many baptisms were performed daily. Father Frois and a number of the padres who had arrived of late from Kyushu had already been dispatched to other cities in the Gokinai provinces.

172

In the mountains, the cherry blossom was at its peak, and bright green fields of barley spread as far as the eye could see. Along the roads, however, the earth was dry, and the wind sent the dust dancing and swirling. I see now that this moment of high springtime marked the zenith of the Signore's reign. But this is clear only from a distance, and after his untimely death, for at the time it seemed that he would not rest until he had scaled even greater heights. Now, all these years later, it seems to me indeed that this radiant spring of fifteen eighty-one was the one truly grand and colorful episode of his reign.

The culmination of these happy days was a splendid and quite unforgettable cavalcade mounted on the parade grounds to the east of the *palazzo* in Kyoto. Our invitation, arriving on the day after the present of the ducks, informed us that the display was to include all the horsemen under the Signore's command. The prospect of such a treat so appealed to the populace that the more impatient were already gathering in the viewing area, though the event was still several days away.

For the occasion, a long alley was constructed running north and south through the parade ground. It was lined on the eastern side with viewing stands for the nobles and on the west with galleries for the commoners. The posts dividing the alley from the stands had been wrapped in scarlet cloth, and pennants and banners fluttered in the wind. The flags were black, red, and lavender, and each was emblazoned with the white crest of one of the *daimyo* lords who had sent riders to the parade. Though the construction had been hasty, the galleries for the nobles, at least, were of considerable splendor, with gold and silver fittings, a beautiful thatched roof, and flowing curtains, much as if a small palace built in a garden had been moved as it stood to the parade ground.

From early morning on the day of the festival, rows of men in green, lavender, and scarlet robes stood up around the central gallery, each wearing a black cap. Lorenzo explained that they were civil officials of the court in Kyoto who had come in attendance on the Dayri, the figurehead emperor who made his home in the capital. The Dayri himself was a small, pale young man who blinked incessantly. From time to time he would whisper something to the principal attendant who sat at his elbow.

We had been provided with seats near this central gallery. Valignano sat between Organtino and Frois in one row, with Lorenzo and the other padres behind them. With clear, calm eyes Valignano surveyed the Buddhist priests, *daimyos*, *governatores*, and generals who filled the galleries on one side, and the commoners opposite them. It was an enormous crowd—more than two hundred thousand, someone said—and people had come all the way from the eastern provinces to be present.

The sun was barely up when we arrived, and long, vertical shadows still shrouded the parade ground, but presently a soft light began to stream into the galleries and with it a fresh breeze blew up. Pennants were unfurled throughout the area, and the neighing of horses could be heard in the distance. Then the *taiko* drums began beating to announce the arrival of the Signore. As he appeared, I confess I gasped in surprise—for his retainers were carrying the red velvet armchair that Valignano had presented to him only a few days since. He had it placed in the center of the gallery, and seated himself to receive salutations from the various dignitaries in attendance.

Before long, people noticed and began to comment on the fact that the Signore was seated in a chair—a present, moreover, from the foreigners. Soon, people were whispering to each other all over the viewing stands. A spectator seated behind us went so far as to ask Lorenzo, albeit quietly, to confirm that the chair was the one Valignano had given the Signore. Lorenzo translated what he could catch of these conversations to give us some notion of the sensation the chair was causing.

"Some," he added, "are even saying that the chair is the Signore's way of announcing that he will presently embrace the Christian faith."

Almost inevitably, the eyes of the crowd focused on the tall and stately Valignano, but he met their gaze with apparent calm. It seemed that even before Lorenzo had spoken Valignano had divined the nature of their reaction, had realized that it was caused by a simple armchair to which no one had hitherto given any particular thought, and the realization had set his mind to work. His clear eyes were shining. Ever since that first meeting in Kuchinotsu, he had opposed Cabral's policies and agreed with Organtino that the priorities of the mission should focus on the capital and Gokinai rather than Kyushu. Yet in fact, though he had come to the capital in response to Organtino's request, he did not really appreciate the significance of missionary work there as much as his unequivocal statement would suggest. In all likelihood, this had been largely motivated by a political need to undermine Cabral's influence rather than by any true understanding of the realities of the situation in the Japanese kingdom. Now, however, when he saw how something as trivial as an armchair could send a tremor through the whole land if brought into proximity with the Signore, he could hardly fail to be impressed with the latter's importance. Many times later he was to refer to his feelings on this occasion, and the fact that following the parade he hurried back to Azuchi to be close to the Signore is proof, perhaps, of how deeply the Signore had imprinted himself on his awareness.

The cavalcade began directly after the Signore had taken his seat. The neighing of horses and hoofbeats were heard, then suddenly, to the beat of a great drum, the first company appeared at the northern end of the parade ground. The horses were fitted with banners that fluttered as they galloped forth. The riders wore shining gold helmets and armor. Their robes were scarlet, and the horses beneath them were decked out in crimson bridles and saddles. Ranks of these marvelous knights charged the length of the alley in perfectly even rows, as if linked by invisible poles: a first, then a second, third, and fourth. The thunder of hoofs set the stands trembling, and a thick cloud of dust swirled up. Something between a cheer and a sigh of admiration arose spontaneously from two hundred thousand throats, then swelled to a thunderous roar. As the final rank came level with the stands, the dust was so thick that the riders were dim shapes, with only the gold of their helmets sparkling through the haze.

The first company cleared the parade ground and the second appeared at the entrance. As the crowd caught sight of this new group, there were more cries of wonder and admiration, for the hundred new riders were all mounted on horses of snowy white. The horses carried pennants of a deep blue; their riders were clad in robes to match, with armor and helmets of iron. Bridles, harnesses, and saddles were blue as well. Grouping themselves in the shape of a diamond, with two horses in the lead, followed by a rank of four, then six, and so on, they streaked through the cloud of dust.

A *samurai* seated near our party was charged with explaining the affiliation of each company to Lorenzo, who in turn relayed the information to Valignano. Soon, a third troop appeared wearing robes of gold brocade with black caps much like those worn by the officials of the Dayri. Their horses, too, were all fitted with gold trappings. As they dashed along, they changed formation with great fluidity, the left crossing over the right and back again, vertical files becoming horizontal and vice versa. After them came several smaller companies of ten to thirty riders, each with horses and men in distinctive costumes of lavender, green, or yellow.

As they came level with the spot where the Signore was sitting, the soldiers of one group slid from their saddles and ducked down on the opposite side so that it appeared that riderless horses were passing the stand. Another company broke formation in the center of the parade ground and rode in single file at full speed past a target that had been set up facing the Signore's stand. One after another, its members drew arrows from their quivers and fired. Despite the speed of the horses, the small target was thick with arrows when they had done. At last, only one rider—no more than a youth—remained to shoot, and as he charged through the dust toward the target and readied his bow, there was an almost palpable tension in the crowd. His arrow was let fly; it, too, found its mark. An explosion of admiration shook the stands.

One group had concentrated on splendid costumes embroidered with gold and silver thread, another sported rainbow-colored bridles shot through with gems and beads. Yet other groups displayed extraordinarily skillful horsemanship, with ever-changing formations; one of them, forming up in several circles, navigated a series of obstacles at a great pace, another created a figure of eight in charging horses that was particularly fine.

The man who had been providing Lorenzo with a commentary on the proceedings explained that these companies were all commanded by their respective generals, and represented the Signore's whole army with the exception of those under the command of Lord Hashiba, at present doing battle with the Mori in the west. Each army vied with the rest, sparing no expense to equip itself in the utmost splendor. The company on white horses, for example, had searched the whole realm for mounts which it purchased solely for the sake of the few moments they spent galloping the length of the parade ground.

Even after the parade had ended and the Signore had retired, many spectators remained in the stands; to them, the wonderful spectacle must have seemed like a beautiful apparition that passes all too quickly. Our own feelings were much the same.

And yet, for me, on the martial figures of these splendid charging riders there lay, inevitably, shadows of the fell warriors and dark deeds I had witnessed during my years in the kingdom of Japan. I recalled the grim sights of the subjugation of Nagashima and the siege of Ishiyama. It was only some ten years since I made the journey from Sakai to Kyoto, but in that time great changes had taken place in the Signore's world. Then all had been in chaos, but gentle and trustworthy Wada and crusty old Araki had still been with us. Kubo-sama had held sway in Kyoto, brooding over his schemes to entrap the Signore. Powerful, hostile armies had been massed to the north of the lake and a great enemy threatened from the east. But all that had passed by in a moment. As the brilliant horsemen had galloped away, so time too had fled, leaving only an empty parade ground.

I would not be surprised if similar thoughts had occurred to Organtino and Father Frois as they sat in the stands that day, but for the Visitor-General, it seems, the spectacle had a very different significance. During the cavalcade—Organtino told me afterward—Valignano had begun to envision a great parish to the east of India with the kingdom of Japan and the Signore at its center.

Organtino himself adopted a flexible approach to his proselytizing activities, now separating politics and religion, now combining them as the occasion required. Valignano—perhaps due to his patrician upbringing—had set his heart on the ambitious notion of a huge parish covering half the globe, and he was not likely afterward to relinquish either the idea or his ties to the Signore upon whom the plan depended. During the long voyage from Goa, as he stared at the blue sea, he had recalled the reports he had read on the mission in Japan, and already, it seems, had indulged in making plans for this land. Then, arriving in Kyushu and beginning his rounds of inspection, he had found, somewhat to his surprise, that the people possessed a most keen intelligence, and a refinement of manner and custom, together with a civility, quite surpassing that of the peoples of Europe. Later, when he had occasion to lecture at the *seminario* in Azuchi, he often made reference to these early impressions, and expressed the opinion that one might search the universities of Bologna, Salamanca, and Coimbra in vain for students as earnest or as clever as those at our school. Finding a people of such unexpected promise, he said, he felt as though part of his dream were already realized. And his decision to take the opposite approach to Cabral's and establish religious schools and seminaries and novitiates throughout the country, so as to train native Japanese friars, was part of the same dream.

At this point he had left Kyushu and come to the capital. He had met the Signore, and had seen the great parade. And he had finally realized that his daydream had every chance of becoming a firm reality. And with reality thus within his grasp, I felt sure that Valignano was unlikely to rest until he had seized it. The energy that drove him was different from the simple devotion that seemed to motivate Frois and Organtino; it was a need to purge his infamous past in the burning activity of the present—a need I could understand all too well.

Valignano seemed never to be at rest. He was constantly absorbed in some project: drawing up a detailed syllabus for use at the *seminario*, convening meetings of a committee to compile a grammar of the Japanese language, creating a daily schedule for the students and teachers at the school, studying the system by which missionaries were dispatched to the various Gokinai provinces. When not engaged in one of these projects, he was closeted with Lorenzo, working on a Latin primer in Japanese or refining a system of musical education.

Valignano had been in indifferent health prior to his arrival in Sakai, and at first his complexion had been somewhat sickly and dark, but by the time we arrived in Azuchi, his natural ruddy coloring had returned. I could still detect traces of weariness on his face, no doubt from long nights spent in penitent labors. Yet the very weariness was a sign of his desire to consume himself in work, to test his own limits, and whenever I saw his exhausted face, I felt a certain closeness that I felt with none of his colleagues. As he set out to follow the Signore to Azuchi, it had seemed to me that his obsession with the dream of a great eastern mission had become an almost physical distress.

The Signore, for his part, greeted Valignano in Azuchi with a show of friendship that was all but inexplicable unless one supposed that he had somehow divined the true nature of the Visitor's troubled existence. The two men, it seemed, had rapidly achieved a deep mutual understanding and respect. With his keen intuition, Valignano had perceived the Signore's isolation and his sense of mission—realized, perhaps, that this lord's path was similar to the road he himself had been treading since that bloody day in Padua. The Signore, on his side, seemed drawn to this man in way he had not been to Organtino or Frois: Valignano, like himself, wielded real power, possessed true breadth of vision. He did not, of course, know of Valignano's dissolute youth or the despair that had followed. He did not know, to be sure, that this man of stern moral precepts had once lain bound in the prison of Venice for cutting up the face of a young woman. Yet it seemed at times as though the Signore had guessed his every secret.

When, for example, the Signore would stop at the *seminario* on his way home from falconing, he would occasionally speak to Valignano about the sorrows of youth. Some men, he said, are overcome by solitude while they are yet too young even to realize it; his own violent deeds, he confessed, might well be due to just such a terrible loneliness. . . . In all that he said on such occasions, he seemed to imply that in Valignano he was addressing a man who might share such feelings.

The day after Valignano arrived in Azuchi, the Signore invited him to the *castello* along with Organtino, Father Frois, Lorenzo, myself, and others. As I have told you, we had already seen the palace, but on this occasion we were treated to a much more extensive tour that included the storehouses, the stables, and even the great kitchen. The latter was equipped to cook for several hundred people at once. Enormous ovens, cupboards, worktables, and sinks were ranged about the wooden floor. High up in the ceiling, a square window provided ventilation.

Next, we made our way out to the stables. Just as we were doing so, several of the white horses that had attracted such attention at the parade were being led in, having been brought by boat across the lake from Kyoto. The Signore stroked the muzzle of each in turn as he questioned Valignano about European horses and horsemanship. The Visitor-General was unstinting in his praise for the riders in the cavalcade and their mounts, but added that in matters of physique, power, and training, European horses were of much higher quality. At this, the Signore launched a barrage of questions, which Valignano, thanks to a keen interest in equestrian matters in his former life, was able to answer admirably, particularly concerning the finer points of size, build, color and gloss of coat, methods of training, breeding, and the like.

As he spoke, we were walking slowly along a long, covered passageway leading to the seven-story keep, the Signore listening intently while Lorenzo and Father Frois interpreted.

"I would like to have some of these European horses brought to Japan as soon as possible," he said at last. "An armed company on such mounts would be a powerful weapon. I must have such horses brought to my kingdom." As he said this, the Signore glanced in my direction as if assuming my collaboration in such a scheme. My immediate reaction, to be honest, was to wonder whether any horse would be able to withstand the long and sweltering journey through the South Seas, let alone the months at anchor in steamy harbors. Even so, I felt a strong urge to respond positively to the Signore's enthusiasm. The desire to have horses of such high reputation was something like his need to see Saint Peter's Basilica with his own eyes. The abstract was merely that—abstract; Saint Peter's magnificence was a thing that gained credence—gained meaning—only when seen. In the same way, horses must be owned, ridden. . . .

As I recall it, the talk between Valignano and the Signore as we made our way up the seven stories of the donjon that day was mainly about the great buildings of Europe: its cathedrals, castles, and palaces. Valignano allowed that the Azuchi *castello* was in no sense inferior to the grandest of European castles, and that in all its fittings and decorations it was a masterpiece of the first rank. The compliment, coming from such an esteemed visitor, did not fail to make an impression on the Signore, who later, in discussing, say, the fortifications, would often refer to Valignano's words.

Around this time or even somewhat earlier, the Signore had hit upon the idea of having a detailed plan of the castle drawn up for presentation to Valignano. It seemed to disturb him that, despite all the talk of the glories of Saint Peter's, no one had been able to produce accurate plans to substantiate the claims. And he was determined to avoid the same pitfall when the time came for the fathers to speak of the Azuchi castle in their homeland. If there were no plans, how would people be able to imagine its splendor? Even as he saw us off that day he had, I am sure, already resolved to commission some.

I find it difficult to explain the ways in which the Signore's friendship for Valignano differed from his friendship with Organtino and his longstanding acquaintance with Frois. Suffice it to say that he held a grand salute to Valignano on his departure, at which he presented him with a magnificent folding screen bearing the above-mentioned plan of the castle painted in quite extraordinary detail. This surely went well beyond anything called for in honor of a Visitor-General come briefly to inspect his church's mission. Such kindness is inexplicable unless the Signore had in fact divined that Valignano, for whatever reason, shared with him the loneliness that came of a determination to test the limits of human existence. I have said more than once that the Signore felt an unspoken kinship with those who sought in their thoughts and actions to follow the dictates of reason, being willing, to that end, to deny their own ego. The patient suffering, the steadfastness, of Frois and Organtino were marks, as it were, of this approach to life, and the affinity with myself that I sensed in the Signore derived from the burning intensity that every moment of his daily existence seemed to convey.

Yet this particular friendship was entirely a matter of tacit understanding, the kind of empathy that grows still deeper as the two individuals grow more solitary, as each confronts more directly the dark void. Valignano's exterior concealed a desperation quite different from Organtino's easygoing cheerfulness and Frois's objective observation. His missionary activities were a moment-to-moment conquest of despair. In him, faith was not something stable and static, but a matter of ceaseless, almost violent, physical and mental activity, as if he were struggling endlessly, desperately, with his past.

Despite his correct and impassive bearing, this massive man with the clear gaze was in a state of constant internal crisis. And the Signore, as a kindred soul, was apparently drawn to the Visitor because he had seen through to this inner struggle. He once told me as much, in fact, and I marveled at his intuition, since I am sure he never learned anything definite of Valignano's earlier years. Nor was he privy to the sight of Valignano in his room at the back of the mission, a telling picture that I can still recall quite clearly. His lamp burned late into the night as he wrote reports on the parish in his elaborate script, or worked over pedagogical projects, doctrinal statements, and practice books for the students learning church music. Occasionally, I would see him thus, and know that the man I saw was not simply hard at work but was doggedly wrestling with something—his own soul, perhaps?

Once the curriculum for the *seminario* was established on the lines of Valignano's plans, we started classes. When it came to the practical business of teaching, however, it was the friendly, loquacious Organtino who proved most adept. As principal of the academy, he lived with the students. He made it a practice, for example, to encourage them to carry on even their most mundane daily conversation in Latin. Thanks to such pedagogical devices, there were several students who could compose Latin prose in no way inferior to the efforts of European students. Though this success did not seem to surprise Organtino himself, it did, apparently, touch him deeply. One evening, reading aloud to us from some of his students' compositions, he became so overcome with emotion that he was unable to continue. He was struck, he said later, by the thought that this distant kingdom was at last beginning to reach a spiritual parity with the Christian nations of Europe. When such talk arose at table, however, Valignano generally disagreed with Organtino's assessment.

"To be sure, the progress you have achieved is remarkable," he would say in his low and measured tones, "but we must keep in mind that true faith is not simply a matter of understanding with the mind. It must be lived every moment. It must be breathed with every breath, one must inhale the spirit of truth with one's whole being. How much more these people might understand— how much more richly they might partake of the mysteries of the faith—if they were given the chance to live amidst the wonders of Rome, Coimbra, Bologna, or Salamanca! I have been painfully aware, of late, that the education we can provide here is sadly restricted."

This conviction that something was lacking in the atmosphere of the *seminario* did not, nevertheless, cause Valignano to lose interest in the place or its work, but seemed rather to spur him on to attempt to compensate for the deficiency. He seemed to have concluded that there was only one means of elevating the spiritual level of the kingdom to the sublime: through music. According to him, only music was capable of instantly creating a rich spiritual atmosphere irrespective of place. It was for this reason that he put so much energy into improving his skill at the organ; music, he maintained, possessed a power to transport the listener to a higher spiritual plane.

There were, at that time, twenty-five young men submitting themselves to the rigors of life at the *seminario*. They wore identical gray robes, spoke little, and almost invariably maintained a most serious demeanor. Occasionally, on a Sunday walk in the countryside or while they were swimming in the lake, there would be hints of the cheerfulness of youth in their voices, but otherwise they were restrained and studious. They laughed little at the jests I would attempt during my lectures, their calm dignity at such times reminding me that, as sons of great warlords, they had received the most serious sort of education. Yet there was something else too at work in their manner. It was almost as though they were constantly conscious of the enormity of the task with which they had been charged, and of their duty as recipients of this special education. Their seriousness inevitably reminded me of Lord Araki's innocent grandchildren who had been executed in Kyoto. Often, looking into the faces of my students, I saw those brave young people who had gone so calmly to meet their death. I should have mentioned that the young men at the *seminario* were for the most part the sons of Takayama's principal retainers.

When time allowed, the Signore would stop in at the mission, where he would sometimes gaze at the Italianate belfry and the fine tiling of the roofs and proclaim:

"We have built Europe here in Azuchi!"

He would often sit listening to music performed by the students, and once commented that he could sense in this foreign music a complicated kind of beauty. These visits, as I have suggested, were due in part to a desire for the familiar company of Frois and Organtino, though certain people at court maintained that his patronage of the mission was only the latest chapter in the Signore's well-known and unending search for novelty. But I am still convinced that their idle chatter missed the point—there was something at a deeper level that drew the Signore.

The Visitor-General had not been long in Azuchi when he set out once again. He returned to Kyoto, then traveled to Takayama's castle to begin a tour of Gokinai. His task was to examine the state of the mission in its entirety, to which end he needed to see as much of its activity as possible.

By the time he had finished his journey and returned to the seminary, summer was beginning and the trees in the mountains around Azuchi were deep green. The lake rippled blue and clear under the summer sky. The schedule of lessons at the seminary had been relaxed somewhat for the summer, and on Organtino's orders more time for swimming and recreation had been allowed for the afternoon hours. Perhaps he recalled the pleasant summer days of his own youth in the countryside of Brescia.

"They are still just boys," he said, a kindly smile playing on his lips as he mopped the sweat from his brow.

On his return, Valignano seemed, once again, less than enthusiastic about Organtino's policy, but when he saw the tanned faces of the boys and the healthy pleasure they took in the recreation, he refrained from expressing his opinion. Even so, he could not resist making it quite clear that the relaxed schedule was to end with the end of summer.

It was shortly after Valignano's return that I learned he would be leaving Japan altogether in the near future. I had sensed a certain impatience in him for some time; he was still the calm, purposeful character I have described heretofore, but now there was a sense of urgency, a suggestion that he needed to be on the move again. Apparently he was anxious to return to Kyushu as soon as possible, and thence to Rome itself by the next available ship.

Organtino told me that when Valignano informed the Signore that he would be leaving, the Signore's first words were:

"But we will surely meet again?"

Valignano assured him absolutely that he was only leaving so suddenly in order to be able to return to Japan again. It was at this interview that the folding screen with the plan of Azuchi castle was presented to Valignano, the Signore pointing out enthusiastically that the plan included not only the castle but the mission hall as well.

Because of the number of stops he would make at churches along the way, it was determined that Valignano should leave Azuchi during the first week of August. On hearing of this, however, the Signore sent a message:

"I would be most grateful if you could postpone your departure for ten days or so. I hope to be able to provide a suitable spectacle as a memento of your stay in Azuchi."

We were at a loss as to what he could be planning. Days passed, and a look of impatience and irritation appeared on Valignano's face. He would pace around the courtyard of the mission hall, stopping at a window from time to time to glance toward the blue-tiled roof of the donjon rising above a sea of green leaves. He would listen for a moment to the trio playing in the music room—organ, viola da gamba, and rebec—then suddenly stalk off to his room to write out some document in his painstaking hand. All arrangements for his departure were complete, and baggage for Frois and Organtino, who were to accompany him as far as Sakai, was also ready, but still no word as to when he might actually set forth had come from the Signore.

We were at breakfast one clear morning in the middle of August when a Christian *samurai*, not unknown to us, brought word from the castle:

"I am sorry to have kept you waiting so long. This evening at dusk the festivities will begin. I hope you will enjoy yourselves."

That afternoon, I went bathing at the lake with the students, and as we passed through the town we saw that the streets had been decorated with flowers and lanterns. From within the castle walls, the sound of firecrackers announcing the beginning of festivities was heard, and throughout the town large crowds had begun to gather in the streets for the merrymaking. There were tent shows, and men were hawking their wares. Drums were beating and bells ringing.

By the time we returned from the lake, the merriment had reached feverpitch, and crowds of gaily dressed women thronged every street. The markets were so full that it was virtually impossible to pass. Organtino told us that word of the festivities had traveled all the way to Kyoto and that people were gathering from all the surrounding areas to see the sight.

As the splendid colors of a summer sunset faded from the sky beyond the Azuchi hill, a deep, radiant dusk spread over the town from the lake. The Signore had personally decreed that not a single candle or lantern was to be lit that evening, and the only light to be seen was the pale flickering of fireflies as they flew off to the lake. On every corner and in every doorway, people waited with bated breath; there were whispers of speculation, but no one in all the town knew exactly what would happen next.

I am not sure how long we waited, but just as the suspense was beginning to wear on us, seated as we were on the balcony of the mission, a single flare suddenly slithered into the sky above the castle and exploded with a loud pop that echoed across the lake. At this signal, the whole *castello* rose out of the darkness all at once, brightly illuminated. We gasped in admiration at the sight—hundreds, perhaps thousands of fires had been lit simultaneously, setting the Azuchi hill ablaze with a reddish light, and along the eaves of each roof of the seven-story tower lanterns had been hung, so that the great castle seemed literally painted in light.

A stir went through the town, and we realized that the enormous crowd of onlookers had begun to run through the darkened streets in the direction of the castle. But before they had got very far, the spectacle grew more extraordinary still as torches flared up in succession, tracing the road from the castle to the mission, exactly as if a great fuse were burning.

As the lines approached us, we could just make out the figures of men, clad all in black and brandishing torches, on either side of the road.

Then, the next instant, the gates of the castle opened like the bursting of a dam, and more black torchbearers came pouring forth in a stream of light that flowed down the hill to the gates of the mission. As each rider reached the end of the path, he extinguished his torch and faded into the darkness, but more riders continued to issue from the gate, so that the river of fire coursed down to us for nearly half an hour.

The effect resembled nothing so much as a colossal fire dragon writhing on the hill; yet as we stood staring, quite dumbfounded, a still brighter mass of flame burst from the gate and shot like an arrow along the path of light, stopping just before our balcony. We could hardly believe our eyes as we discovered the Signore astride his horse at the heart of this blaze. He was clad all in black, and held a torch raised in salute to Valignano.

I still recall Valignano's departure most vividly. I accompanied the party as far as a small town on the shore of the lake, some distance from Azuchi, but since I was to act as agent for the school in Organtino's absence, I was obliged to part with them there and return to Azuchi that night. Valignano clasped my hand firmly. He supposed, he said, that he would never forget his wonderful sojourn in this kingdom. He was returning to see to various pressing matters, but hoped we would meet again in the future.

He moved off into the distance, surrounded by twenty or so of the faithful who were to see him to Sakai. The burning sky of the late summer evening set fire to the lake, and the golden clouds were like flames. I stood watching as his figure shrank to a point then vanished on the far shore, and still I stood as the glow of the sunset faded and twilight crept into the fields and paddies, over the woodlands and the highway. As Valignano went, it seemed to me that a brightness and brilliance went with him.

In the days that followed, I made my way, once my classes were finished, through the town and to the lakeshore. With the end of the summer festivals all was quiet again; except for the children playing in the water, nothing remained of lightness and celebration. In the wind that blew down from Azuchi hill, I could feel the dryness of autumn.

The seasons were changing, but the stalemate continued in the battle with the Mori army to the west, and more than one spy had reported that the Takeda army was likely to take advantage of this situation to attack the Signore from the rear. After seven long years, the Takeda had, it seemed, finally managed to recover from the wounds they had suffered at the battle of Nagashino. The Signore, however, had resolved to attack the Mori with all his resources and was unperturbed by these reports. His confidence in Hashiba, commanding the army to the west, was apparently complete, and in addition he could now rely on the allegiance of Ieyasu for protection from Takeda. Barring a treacherous move by this new ally, he should have ample defenses to the rear—and we were assured that the Signore had taken various steps to ensure Ieyasu's loyalty.

In the early spring of fifteen eighty-two, when the Signore's forces invaded Shinano in pursuit of Takeda, it was Ieyasu who formed the advance guard. The Signore launched a relentless series of attacks on the Takeda fortresses, driving deep into the land known as Kainokuni and destroying the Takeda army wherever it offered resistance. As in previous campaigns, the enemy, foot soldier and great general alike, was put to the sword, and mounds of corpses were left in the wake of the Signore's army. The Signore issued a proclamation to his troops:

"Should even a single soldier of the Takeda army escape with his life, may your shame be too great for you ever to return to your homes." The reports of the battle reaching Azuchi described deeds no less grim and ghastly than those that accompanied the fall of Nagashima. In my mind's eye I could see the Signore standing amidst smoke and flame, staring off in the direction of the enemy lines, the expression on his pale face much like Valignano's as he set out for distant Rome. Since his imprisonment in Venice, Valignano had suffered from occasional violent headaches which left his face with an underlying pallor not unlike the Signore's. Both men, too, shared this habit of gazing off at some point, some distant truth visible to their eyes alone. Perhaps their's was an expression common to men who, in the face of great personal suffering and the vagaries of history, stake their whole beings on bringing some notion or principle to concrete fruition. That was what I, at least, saw in their faces.

Others offered different interpretations. In the Signore's case, some of his closest advisers took his cool, tense expression as a sign of imperturbable cruelty. Likewise, there were those among the friars who felt Valignano's reserve and aloofness to be due to hidden ambition. In both cases, however, I would disagree. Valignano had a past to live with, and the Signore, I think, was more consistent than cruel. If he judged men harshly, if he had no patience even with the gentle, refined Sakuma, it was not from meanness of spirit, but from a desire to confront each challenge with strictness and strength—and to have others do the same.

In the stern reprimand issued at the time of Sakuma's banishment, he had, conversely, praised two of his generals whose actions he contrasted with Sakuma's weakness. The two were, of course, the well-loved Hashiba and Lord Akechi. Hearing Organtino translate the articles of the reprimand, it occurred to me that these two very different men—one so cheerful and the other so cool and reserved—were perhaps the only friends remaining to the Signore among his countrymen.

The Signore often spoke of them, but, not being one to reveal himself in conversation, rarely did more than compliment them as masters of the art of war. I would guess, however, that his sympathy for them lay in the perception that, in following the path of the warrior, they too had encountered a solitude not unlike his own. They did, indeed, seem to share a certain resolve and sternness that set them apart from other men.

That was perhaps all they shared, for they were in other matters quite different. Hashiba favored lively banquets and splendid, even gaudy interiors, while Akechi preferred sedate pastimes such as reading in the solitude of his study. Yet both possessed a quality that appealed to the Signore above all others—the ability to do the necessary thing to achieve the desired end without any sign of emotion, with neither hesitation nor compunction.

It seems to me now somewhat curious that I was not particularly familiar with either Hashiba or Akechi. My only personal recollection concerning Akechi dates from about the time the court was removed to Azuchi. I remember being rather surprised and a trifle mystified at a request he made to Organtino for some Latin books. But I soon learned the explanation; it was on behalf of one of his daughters who was known for her belief in Christianity. I suppose my initial surprise had been due to the improbability of a man of Akechi's intellect and temperament being attracted by the Christian view of things. In this sense he was very like the Signore. Not that either man was insensitive; the Signore, for example, greatly cherished the subtle beauty of the utensils used to drink the brew the Japanese call *cha*, and, as you have seen, he could be moved by the sight of a cripple by the side of the road. And yet, in war, he was capable of the most callous strategies in the name of lucid, rational thought. In a sense, both the Signore and Akechi bore the scars of battles fought in the name of rationality.

Yet it seems unlikely that Akechi, personally, was entirely lacking in sympathy with the Christian type of compassion. Although he was capable of prosecuting his grim military strategies with an efficiency rivaling the Signore's own, it could not be imagined that he shared the Signore's censorious attitude toward those such as Lord Sakuma who were relatively mild and lenient. He was, it seems, of two minds in this matter. While he might criticize Sakuma as a general and strategist, he also loved him as a man—all the more, perhaps, because of his susceptibility to the milder emotions. The fact that the banishment of Sakuma wounded Akechi more deeply than any of the other vassals was due not only to his close ties to the Christian faction, but to a sense that his own simple human affections had been mercilessly repudiated. No doubt the blow was even greater coming, as it did, close on the heels of Araki's disastrous rebellion. Both Sakuma and Araki had been closely associated with his own state of mind, and the two events, clearly, deeply saddened him.

If Akechi had always found it difficult to live up to the Signore's stern demands—in particular his requirement that Akechi join him in the icy void—then after the loss of these two friends he almost certainly found it doubly difficult, doubly lonely. And it seems that he wearied of this struggle to hold the line, grew sick of dangling above the abyss of solitude. No doubt he had long since been weary. Who can say? All these years later, as I try to imagine what must have been in his heart, I cannot shake off the notion that he felt himself pursued by watchful, accusing eyes—eyes that urged him, goaded him ever further and higher along a lonely path. So long as the eyes followed him, he could not rest. . . .

It was a spring evening in fifteen eighty-two when the Signore's forces returned to Azuchi from their victory over the Takeda. The town was buzzing with excitement. Saké had been distributed in honor of the triumph, and after drinking deeply, the men paraded through the streets carrying the shrines of the gods of this country. A flood of people swirled and eddied about them, calling out, singing, and making merry. Young men and women had spread mats beneath the rows of cherry trees on the outskirts of the town, and sat filling one another's cups while beating time for the dancers. I was heading back to the *seminario*. On my way, I passed troops marching along the highway. By the banners they carried, I recognized the soldiers of Lord Akechi's army, and beyond them I could see the generals approaching slowly on horseback. At the head of this group was Akechi himself.

Suddenly, the army was engulfed by the crowd, and cries of adulation for the returning conquerors swept the street. The soldiers nodded acknowledgment as they passed, some of them already holding hands with wives or sweethearts. Every face was cheerful, the eyes sparkling with the joy of returning alive and victorious.

I will never forget, however, the one face in that crowd that was neither flushed nor satisfied—that of Lord Akechi. Alone amidst the gaiety, his expression was grim and set. He seemed lost in thoughts of his own, and would look up from time to time as if startled to find himself in such a place, among such a raucous crowd.

"They are all dancing," he seemed to be thinking, "singing, drinking, making love. They have no more serious worry than where they might borrow some money, or how to mend a lovers' quarrel. Nothing is driving them; their days pass in peace. Summer follows spring, autumn summer, till winter comes and their lives, like the brief red evening sun, fade into darkness. How I envy them! How deeply and sweetly they must sleep! How different my nights, when the least puff of wind sets my nerves on edge and I listen for distant hoofbeats. I too would sleep their dreamless sleep. How weary I am. . . . But those eyes! Always watching me! Even on the darkest night, still they are watching me. And I am not even sure what it is they want. Is it hatred I see in them? Or contempt? No, not exactly. Not malice either, nor scorn: I think I could accept those. No—I fear the look is one of fellow-feeling . . . some deep, private sense of complicity. It is *that* that drives me along this road, that drives me up this mountain. So as long the eyes follow me, I have no choice but to climb ever higher into the cold, empty sky. No choice but to seek perfect mastery in my chosen field. . . .

"But now my strength is gone at last. I can climb no higher. I want only to sleep, to fall headlong into the sweetness of oblivion . . . like snow on a silent winter's night . . . falling to the bottom of the world. . . ."

You may think this soliloquy fanciful, but it is no fancy that Akechi left the court in Azuchi almost immediately after his arrival and made for his castle in Sakamoto. He excused himself by saying that he was terribly weary and wished only to sleep. His complaint was generally regarded as battle fatigue, but I, who saw his face as he rode through the streets in triumph, do not believe it was just that.

At the end of May in that same year, I was called to Kyoto by Father Frois. The weather was abnormally warm and humid the day before I was to set out, and though I taught my classes, my whole body had felt flushed and languid, rather as it had just before I was taken with a fever in the jungles of Nuova Spagna. I had intended to retire early and leave for Kyoto at dawn, but instead spent the following day resting in bed, my body shaken by the reverberation of the organ beyond the wall. The next day was rainy, but feeling somewhat revived, I wrapped myself in a cloak and set out on horseback. On the highway outside the town, I saw soldiers bustling about in the rain. I supposed they were to join the army due to make a final attack against the stubborn Mori. I watched as they foddered their horses or sheltered under the eaves eating their breakfast. . . .

It was two days later that I learned in Kyoto of Akechi's rebellion. There had been nothing in the faces of the soldiers I had seen on the Azuchi highway to suggest knowledge of what was to come. I learned later that in the days before his treachery Akechi had been in seclusion at a temple on Mount Atago. Perhaps he was praying for release from the sympathetic eyes. Perhaps he hoped to rest. But the Signore had already left Azuchi in the company of thirty or so retainers to ride to Honnoji, and it was clear that nothing had changed. There would be no rest: everything continued to move forward with the inevitability that the Signore so cherished. The army would advance to the west, inexorably, and Akechi would again feel those eyes on him, more fierce, more loving than ever, more sternly demanding that he scale the heights.

But he had had enough. The time had come for him to escape. If only the eyes could be closed forever, he might sleep. If only they would dissolve and vanish, he might slumber. Yes, that was the only solution: the eyes—the eyes that were almost his own—must be blinded, darkened forever. At the very moment I stood watching the soldiers, he must have been staring out at the rain on the green foliage. Everything was in flames, and it was for him to extinguish the fire.

That night I was unable to reach Kyoto, and slept poorly on the unfamiliar bed of a cheap lodging house in that eastern kingdom.

I listened to the rain as I tossed and turned throughout the interminable hours. At dawn, I set out once more. The rain had nearly stopped and a cold wind was chasing the clouds off in the direction of the lake. Beneath the overcast sky I saw that soldiers were again on the move—westward now, along the Azuchi highway.

After that, my friend, things disintegrated rather rapidly. Following the Signore's death and the fire at the Honnoji temple, Akechi had sent his soldiers—the same that I had seen on the highway, perhaps—to raze the splendid castle at Azuchi, and with it the *seminario*. The treacherous rage of Akechi burned briefly across the land, a pale flame soon to be extinguished. Before long, riders were to be seen sweeping through the streets of Kyoto, and Hashiba's army, a relentless tide, sacked castle after castle until the whole land lay in submission. But I could not help feeling that something truly splendid—though ever so fleeting— had been destroyed; even as I write these words to you now, years later beneath the blistering sun of Goa, I can still hear collapse and ruin echoing in the silence surrounding me. . . .

You see, my friend, for me it was not simply a kingdom of the east that was rent asunder in that moment; it was also, I fear, my own soul. Thus you will forgive, and perchance pity, my ten years of idle mourning here in barren India.

It was nearly a year after the Signore's death that I was finally able to board a ship and say farewell to the shores of Japan. The weather that day was warm and clear, and we sailed with the fair wind that the sailors of Genoa call *il vento in poppa*.